"Final Showdown"

M/M Wolf Shifter Mpreg Paranormal Romance

The Cyan Conspiracy Vol 3

Apollo Surge

This book is intended for Adults (ages 18+) only. The contents may be offensive to some readers. It may contain graphic language, explicit sexual content, and adult situations. May contain scenes of unprotected sex. Please do not read this book if you are offended by content as mentioned above or if you are under the age of 18. Please educate yourself on safe sex practices before making potentially life-changing decisions about sex in real life.

This story is a work of fiction. Names, characters, businesses, places, events and incidents are the products of the author's imagination or used in a fictitious manner and are not to be construed as real. Any resemblance to actual persons, living or dead, or actual events is purely coincidental. Products or brand names mentioned are trademarks of their respective holders or companies. The cover uses licensed images and are shown for illustrative purposes only. Any person(s) that may be depicted on the cover are simply models.

Edition v1.00 (2021.04.19)
apollo@apollosurge.com

Special thanks to the following volunteer readers who helped with proofreading: RB, Blue Savannah, and those who assisted but wished to be anonymous. Thank you so much for your support.

Prologue

"You failed to keep your pet on a leash," Dr. Malone spat as she paced back and forth in her office, located in the huge fortress that was Black Gate, a dark place where dark experiments were performed. Hammond sat before her, looking like a scolded child. His hands were in his lap and his head was bowed. His gaze darted towards the door and a cold bead of sweat dripped down the back of his neck, for he worried that the cruel doctor would keep him for one of her experiments. Few people came into Black Gate and left again.

"I tried my best! I don't know what happened. He changed. I couldn't control him."

"It was your job to control him. I sent him to you for a reason Hammond. I arranged for you to become a very rich man, and you have failed to live up to your end of the bargain."

"But it was working! You were getting the results you wanted. He was turning into an animal. I'd never seen anything like it. He was magnificent," Hammond's voice turned into an awed whisper and his eyes shone with the memory of his fighter destroying every opponent that came into the arena.

"And then you let him get away! What were you thinking? You had one job Hammond. I went against my instincts and trusted you. Do not make me regret it." Dr. Malone pointed a slender finger towards Hammond, jabbing it like a dagger. Hammond gulped. Dr. Malone placed her hands on her desk. Dark shadows ringed her eyes and errant strands of hair fell across her face. Her eyes blazed with intense fury.

"They are the key to my work. I need them," her gaze had drifted away from Hammond for a moment, but then it snapped back. "You will get them for me. I want both of them, back here."

Hammond shifted uncomfortably in his seat. "I don't mean to question your judgment, but you have the resources of the entire facility at your disposal. Surely your armed guards would be more suitable for this task than I would be?"

Dr. Malone gave him a withering look. "I thought you were supposed to be smart Hammond. We pride ourselves on our discretion. There is nothing discreet about a squadron of guards rushing through the city ready and willing to abduct two men. No, you must do this for me, otherwise I will find some other way for you to repay your debt."

Her words were laden with threat and Hammond's face paled. He nodded. "Yes, of course, I'll find a way to make it happen. I won't let you down," he stammered before he fled the office, rushing out of Black Gate before he became a prisoner there.

Meanwhile, Dr. Malone walked through the empty halls of her facility and shook her head at the carnage strewn around, all caused by her nephew. It was impressive in a way, but an old familiar resentment burned inside her. It wasn't right that such power should be hoarded by people who didn't deserve it. She followed the trail around to a cage that had been broken open. Dr. Malone placed her hands on her hips and exhaled deeply. It would soon be time for a family reunion. The next time she saw them, she wasn't going to let anything stop her from achieving her ambitions. She had worked too long and too hard to see it all fail now. But with the latest revelation, with news of the child, she knew that the last piece of the puzzle was falling into place. Finally, she would unlock the secrets of her DNA and take the power from the wolves. Finally, she could have her birthright.

But first, she needed the child.

Chapter One

Alex sat in darkness. He breathed heavily, still trying to understand everything that had happened. It wasn't so long ago that his life was simple. He knew nothing other than fighting for Mr. Hammond and he was good at it. He knew his purpose, but there was always something nagging at the back of his mind, something that suggested he was meant for something more. Then he had met Ben and suddenly his world had opened up. He experienced feelings and emotions that he had never experienced before, and Ben had shown him that some monster who deserved to be in chains. He was more than that. Things had only grown more complicated when Ben and his colleague Amelia had started to investigate the Cyan corporation. The information they retrieved had dovetailed with Alex's mind and gradually he started to piece together his memories.

The wolf pack he had been a part of had been captured by Cyan, by a woman he now learned was his aunt. She had also captured Ben, and he might well have died had Alex not saved him. They had also saved Alex's mother as well, but he hadn't been able to save them all, and the guilt weighed heavily on him.

"You look tired," Ben said quietly. The room was filled with shadows. It had been a long night, and the day seemed a long time away. Ben sat beside Alex and rested his head on Alex's shoulder. His hand still trembled. Alex took it, wrapped it in his warmth, and the tremble stopped.

"Are you okay?" Alex asked.

"I'm not sure. Everything seems so surreal. I never really thought of myself coping with a situation like that. I didn't think it could ever happen."

"What was it like?"

"Horrible. I didn't know how long I had been there. I didn't understand what she wanted from me. I was hoping that something would happen, that you would come and save me, but at the same time I was afraid for you as well. I didn't want you to be captured."

"It worked out for the best," Alex said.

"Did it?" Ben looked at him directly. He spoke tersely, although he softened immediately afterwards. "I'm sorry. I'm still trying to process everything that's happened. It doesn't quite make sense to me, and yet at the same time I know it's true. I can feel it inside," he glanced down to his stomach and pressed his hand against his abdomen.

"I didn't know this could happen Ben. I swear to you. I'm sorry. If I had known..."

Ben smiled. "Don't worry about it Alex. It's not like it's bad news, it's just...unexpected is all. I mean, I never thought that this would ever happen. What am I supposed to do?"

"I guess let nature take its course," Alex said, although he knew that it was unhelpful.

"I guess...how are you feeling about it?"

Alex ran a hand across his head and raised his eyebrows. "I'm not entirely sure. Part of me is excited, while another part of me wonders how I'm supposed to take care of a child when I can't even take care of myself."

"You take pretty good care of yourself. I don't think anyone else could have rescued me from that place."

"It's not that…it's just that I don't feel like I know myself. I have more memories back, but they feel like a dream, as though I'm remembering someone else's life. And with all this happening how can I bring a child into the world? What if they just get put in danger like we've been?"

"I don't know, but the dice have been rolled and we can't take them back. I just hope that I can carry this child to term. I mean, is it even possible?"

Alex shrugged. There were still so many things he didn't know, like why his aunt would do such terrible things and betray her family.

"Ben…this isn't over."

"I know."

"I need to get the others back. It's not right that they should be suffering in that place. I need to rescue them."

"They'll be more prepared for an attack next time. I don't think they're going to let you walk in there and free the rest of the wolves."

"I don't know what else to do. All I know is that I need to save them. I feel it, in here," he prodded the middle of his chest. "I feel it deeper than anything else, anything except my feelings for you." Alex looked sheepishly towards Ben, but Ben just smiled and draped his arm around Alex's shoulders.

"You know, I always knew that love was complicated, but I never thought it would be like this," he said with a wry smile. Alex chuckled and nodded. He clasped Ben's hand a little more tightly. "I wish I could promise you that everything was going to turn out okay," he said.

"We can promise each other," Ben said. Alex looked up and their eyes met. He pressed his forehead against Ben's and closed his eyes, enjoying the peaceful moment where the rest of the world could melt away and it could just be the two of them. He inhaled the warm scent of Ben's breath and took comfort in the closeness and the intimacy that reigned between them.

After a few moments, Ben leaned back and glanced towards the door of the spare bedroom.

"When are you going to talk to her? She'll probably have more answers."

"I thought I'd let her rest first," Alex said, turning his gaze away. For so long there had been an image in his mind, a whisper, and now it had been given form. His mother was in a room adjacent to him, close enough to touch, and yet Alex was still reticent to actually go and speak to her.

"You're scared aren't you," Ben said. It was more of an observation than a question.

Alex nodded. "I know I shouldn't be. She's my mom after all, but I just...I don't know. It's been so long..."

"I'm sure she's been missing you. She might have given up on the chance of ever seeing you again. It's natural to be afraid, but I don't think you have any reason to be. And if it does go south, well, you're with the perfect guy who has been through a bad reunion with his mother, and believe me, nothing can be as bad as that."

Alex smiled and breathed in deeply. Ben somehow always knew the right thing to say or do to ease the tension he was feeling. He was overwhelmed with love and couldn't believe his fortune that he had found Ben, against all odds...or perhaps it was that Ben had found him. Either way, they were both lucky. Emotion swelled with Alex's heart.

"I don't know what I would have done if you hadn't come into Hammond's bar that night."

"You'd probably still be fighting," Ben said dryly.

"I'm serious Ben. I wouldn't have had anyone to turn to. Nobody would have believed in me. I would have just been a monster, some beast, and I don't think I ever would have escaped that. I'm not sure my memories would have returned without you."

"I'm glad I had such a positive effect. Just for the record my life is a whole lot better too."

"It is? I mean, you've been kidnapped and tortured and you're also pregnant. I think it's pretty clear who has come off better in this deal," Alex said.

"I don't know…to be honest part of me has always wondered what it would be like to be pregnant. I just hadn't ever thought it would happen. It's going to take a lot of getting used to I think, but I'm not sad that it's happened. I just have to think about the future more." He trailed off for a moment before continuing. "You know Alex, you should go and speak to her. She's probably scared. She's been in that place for so long who knows what they've done to her mind."

"That's what I'm afraid of," Alex said, his gaze drifting towards the closed door. But he knew in his heart that Ben was right. He licked his lips and pushed himself off the couch, giving Ben a kiss before he did so. He walked slowly towards the door and his hand hovered above the handle, before he turned it and walked in.

***

The room was dark. The curtains had been drawn so only a sliver of moonlight poured through. Alex's gaze drifted towards the bed, but it was empty. His brow furrowed. Because of his enhanced senses, a gift of his wolf blood, his vision was better than the average man, so the darkness wasn't such a barrier to him. There she was, hunched and huddled in the corner. Her knees were drawn into her chest and two furtive eyes darted about behind a straggling veil of hair. She trembled and a low growl left her mouth as Alex approached. He held out a hand and moved slowly, walking around the bed. Her gaze never left him.

"It's okay Mom. I know you've been through a lot and this is all probably confusing for you. I just...I want you to know that you can trust me. I was like you for a long time. I didn't know what was happening or what was going on. Hell...I didn't even know who I was. But I remembered, and you can remember too." It tore at his heart to think of his mother being lost in the same abyss as he. Inside he had always assumed that his mother would have all the answers, that she would be stronger than he was and she would be able to help him. But, as it turned out, it was he that needed to be strong for her. His throat ran dry as he thought of the prospect that she would never be able to recover, that the only thing remaining of her would be a memory.

Although she was anxious, she did not try and run, for which he was grateful.

"Think Mom...think back to the lake. I know it's hard but think of everything you told me. You talked about the moon and how that no matter what happened in our lives the moon would always be looking down upon us. You were right Mom. She was looking down on me, and she led me back to you. I've missed you Mom. I've missed you so much. I'm sorry that I didn't come and get you sooner. I'm sorry that it took me so long, but I'm here now. You're here too. We're safe now. We don't have to worry about this any longer."

As he spoke, he gradually worked his way around the bed and closed the distance between them. He kept himself low so as to not appear threatening, and it seemed to be working as his mother did not move an inch. In fact, as he grew closer, she opened his arms a little and looked up at him. The fear in her eyes was diminished. Alex smiled and got on his knees too. He waddled towards her and opened his arms. Her lips were cracked and she was so thin it was unsettling. Her skin was sallow, but the most important thing was that she was alive. She tilted her head back a little and sniffed the air, and then realization spread across her face.

"Alex?" she whispered. A smile broke out upon Alex's face as he wrapped his arms around his mother. She opened her arms to him as well and they were lost in a deep embrace. He buried himself in her hair, and although she had little strength, he felt safe in her arms. The embrace brought forth a lot of forgotten, instinctual memories. There was a part of him that just knew this was where he belonged. By finding and rescuing her he had found a part of himself, a part that he worried had been lost forever.

Chapter Two

Ben watched to door, waiting for Alex to return. He hoped that Alex's reunion with his mother went better than Ben's with his biological mom. The circumstances were different of course. Alex and his mom had been separated against their will. He just hoped that it would be less painful.

He leaned back in the couch and his hands fell against his stomach, gently caressing his abdomen. He stared at himself in disbelief. It still seemed impossible that he should be with child. It went against everything he had ever been taught, and yet in Alex he had already been faced with one impossibility. If werewolves could exist, then why couldn't men get pregnant? Even so, it didn't make it any easier to process. So many wild thoughts whirled through his mind. It was a raging storm that did not seem to cease, and he longed for Alex to return to offer him a sense of calm.

In time he did, and he seemed content.

"She's resting now," Alex said. "But she remembered me. She remembered Ben," he seemed happy. The two of them went to bed and slept. Ben enjoyed feeling the warmth of Alex beside him. It made the world feel safe, but in the depths of his mind, Ben was plagued with feelings of trauma. He could still hear the sneering tone of Dr. Malone whispering to him, telling him everything she was going to do to him. He struggled against the restraints and it felt as though he was still being held in Black Gate. At one point in the night he awoke in a cold sweat, surrounded by darkness. His dream had been so real that he clutched the sheets in terror, afraid that he was still in Black Gate. It took a few moments for him to orient himself and tell himself that it was alright, that Alex had saved him, and he didn't have anything else to fear from that place.

But he always knew that although he might have been done with Black Gate, Black Gate might not be done with him. Dr. Malone coveted what he had and she didn't seem like the type to give up easily. He reached across to his bedside cabinet and drained a glass of water, although he was still thirsty. As his head hit the pillow again his mind was alive with wild thoughts, mostly about the child. There were still so many questions that needed to be answered. The most pertinent one was if he could even be responsible for a child. There was a gnawing fear that he might not be a good parent at all, and that he or she might be better off if they had someone who knew what they were doing. But then he realized that his biological mother must have had the same thoughts. Nausea churned in his stomach at the thought that he was anything like her.

He turned around and forced himself to sleep.

***

The following morning, Ben bid farewell to Alex as he wanted to give Alex the opportunity to be alone with his mom and try to reconnect with her. Besides, Ben had business to attend to with Amelia. He met her in a small diner that was quiet. They took a booth in the corner and spoke low, so that nobody could hear them. Amelia wore a long coat, dark glasses, and a beret. She had also dyed her hair blonde and chopped it short so that it only reached the base of her skull. She slid into the booth and tapped her fingers on the table skittishly, eyes darting around in case anyone should be looking at them.

The only person in close vicinity was the waitress though. The only other customer in the diner was sitting near the door, gazing out of the window.

"I don't think I was followed," Amelia said in a low voice. She took the glasses off and placed them down onto the table. She looked exhausted.

"Did you sleep?" Ben asked.

"Sleep? I have no time for sleep. I couldn't sleep, not after last night. Do you just realize what we did? We woke the beast Ben. We've been marked now."

"Amelia, come on, you're being crazy."

"Crazy? Am I? They had you Ben, and they know that you work with me. It's not going to take them long to put two and two together. We can't trust anyone," as she said this the waitress came over. Amelia eyed her suspiciously and barked an order of coffee. Ben ordered a small breakfast and looked at his friend with worry.

"Amelia, you have to calm down. This isn't going to help anyone."

"Calm down? How can I calm down? I live in a world where evil corporations have mad scientists captured werewolves. How the hell do you expect me to calm down?" She was so worked up that her voice threatened to break free of the whisper. Amelia bowed her head once again and gazed around, hoping that she had not betrayed herself with her outburst.

"Well there's something else that might blow your mind even more. Actually, I'm not sure that I should tell you, just in case you can't handle it."

"Don't do that Ben. Don't keep things from me. Not now. Not after all we've been through," she pointed at Ben and her eyes narrowed. Ben opened his palms and told her everything that happened when he was held prisoner at Black Gate. Amelia stared at him in disbelief. For a moment Ben thought that something had broken inside her because she froze. But then, she smiled.

"Ben, that's...that's something. Congratulations I guess, I mean, it just about fits with all the other crazy stuff that's been going on. Wow, I just...I mean, okay," she said as she tried to come to terms with this herself. Ben understood of course; it was still taking him time to get used to it. "Are you sure this is true though? I mean, what if she was lying to you?"

"Why would she lie?"

"Why would she capture you and tie you up? All I'm saying is that I'm not sure this doctor is a reliable source."

"She's not, but I don't think she'd lie about something like this. And it makes sense. I've been feeling...different lately. I thought it was just the stress of everything that was going on, but now I realize that there's something more. I can feel it inside me. It must be what everyone calls mother's intuition, although in my case I suppose that description isn't entirely accurate."

"No, I suppose it wouldn't be. What are you going to do?" Amelia asked awkwardly. It was a question that had to be asked unfortunately, and one that had been a fleeting presence in his mind, but it was also one that he had been able to answer easily.

"I'm not going to do anything to it, if that's what you mean. This child is a miracle and I can't just stop something like this from happening."

"Well, I guess nobody is really ready to be a parent."

"Yeah, although a little more time to prepare would have been nice," Ben replied with a wry smile.

"How does Alex feel about it all?"

"He seems happy. Like me he's a little confused. There's still lots of things that need to be sorted out though. There's just so much going on we haven't really had a chance to sit down and think about it too much. He's with his mom at the moment. I just hope there's enough of her left to shed some more light on what's been happening."

"Yeah...listen, I don't know if this is the right time to talk about this given what you just told me, but what are we going to tell William?"

"The truth?" Ben asked. "Although I suppose maybe we should think about keeping some things hidden." He exhaled deeply. "I don't know in all honesty."

"The thing is Ben, it's all well and good to write everything we experienced, but who the hell is going to believe us? It's not as though we're the first people to ever go up against big corporate money, and I don't think our chances of winning are very good at the moment."

"No, but I can't just give up either. I don't know what else there is we can do. It's not right that they should get away with this. Part of the reason why I got into journalism was to stop things like this from happening. If we can't fix it then maybe we're part of the problem."

"I just worry that we're biting off more than we can chew."

"I know. Look, I'm not going to put anyone in danger, especially now. Let's head to the office and speak to William. Maybe he knows something we can do, or someone we can contact."

***

They left the diner and made their way to the office. They walked briskly, and Amelia was constantly looking over her shoulder in case anyone was following them. Ben was a little less paranoid, although he couldn't discount the possibility entirely. Ben thought of Alex and how things were going with his mother. Hopefully she would be able to give them some information that would help bring Black Gate down as well.

When they entered the office, William stood in the doorway and beckoned them in.

"What the hell have you two done?" he asked, his face as grim as a storm. Ben and Amelia glanced towards each other and gulped.

Chapter Three

Alex awoke with nerves in his stomach. Ben left to go
and see Amelia, although in truth Alex wouldn't have
minded had he stayed. They were a family now, and
whatever trials and tribulations they faced in life, they
would face them together. He made some breakfast
and took it in on a tray into the bedroom. Sunlight
now poured in through the window, a slanting beam of
light that illuminated everything, including the dust
particles that hung in the room. Alex had hoped that
his mom would have used the bed, but it remained
untouched. He walked around and saw her draped
over the floor, curled into a ball. She had been caged
for so long that she must have forgotten what it was
like to sleep in a normal bed.

"Mom...Mom...it's morning," he said. He placed the tray
on the bed and shook her leg. She awoke with a start
and immediately snarled, drawing her body into a
tight ball. She seemed more animal than human, and
Alex knew that all too well. He remembered how he
had been when Hammond had first trained him to be
a fighter. Alex didn't know anything other than what
his instincts were telling him, and with Hammond
controlling everything around him, his instincts told
him nothing but fear and pain. He wasn't going to let
his mother suffer the same fate. He wanted her
instincts to feel love.

He sat on the bed and smiled, speaking calmly.

"It's okay Mom. You don't have to be afraid. You're
safe. Look, I made you some breakfast." He gestured
to the tray. His mom eyed it suspiciously. Alex moved
back so that he was on the opposite side of the bed.

His mom crawled forward and started to eat, nibbling on the toast and drinking the juice hungrily. Alex watched her with pity, knowing that this was not the way she would have wanted him to see her. Anger burned in his heart for his aunt and all the rest at Black Gate. He wished he would have been able to turn the entire place to rubble, because it was a place of sorrow and malevolence.

"I'm glad you're eating. That's a good sign," he said. He took things slowly and didn't force her to speak or do anything before she was ready. After she ate, he managed to coax her out into the lounge. She twitched and looked around, seeming amazed that the place was so big. It wasn't really, but it must have appeared that way to her considering she had been caged for so long.

Alex continued speaking, settling on the couch while his mom explored the place.

"I have to be honest with you Mom, this isn't how I thought a reunion would go. Damn, she really did a number on you, didn't she? I'm sorry I couldn't rescue you before. I was in trouble myself. Mom, do you remember who I am now?"

His mother turned to him and her eyes went wide, as did her smile. She nodded.

"Alex," she said. Alex smiled, and while she didn't offer much in conversation, he told her everything that he could remember and had experienced since they had been separated. When he talked about that dark night where the pack had been captured his mother shuddered.

"Bad night, bad night, she said. The more time they spent together the more she was regaining her senses and her capacity to communicate. She started to resemble a human more than a wolf, and Alex could breathe a sigh of relief as her shattered, halting words began to form more coherent sentences. She pinched the bridge of her nose and still seemed skittish, leaning forward, curling the ends of her hair. It pained him to see her like this. In his mind he remembered her being graceful and elegant, exuding a calm confidence. Now she was the opposite of that, as though her spirit had been broken. But that was better than her being dead.

"Mom, I've tried to piece together as much as I can from that night, from all of this…but there are still some things I don't understand. How can it be that my aunt would do this? Why don't I have any memory of her? Why would she betray her family, her pack?"

His mother's face was ashen and drawn. She looked so similar to the woman he had seen looming over Ben, the evil doctor. At first, he had been stunned and mistook her for his mother, but then the truth had emerged and she had revealed herself as his aunt. She and his mother were twins, but now it was clear that the two of them were different sides of the same coin. Even though his mother was in such a fraught state, she still had warmth in her eyes, which was more than he thought his aunt Sophie would ever have been capable of.

"It was never her pack, not really," she said in a croaking voice. "At least that's the way she always saw it. She wasn't like me. She never got the wolf gene, and she hated me for it. She hated all of us. She couldn't understand why. She thought somehow she was being punished, that she was less of a person because she wasn't like the rest of us. We never tried to ridicule her for it, but she couldn't accept that she was different. She tried everything. She used to plea with the moon every night. She looked at ancient spells and herbal concoctions, all to try and awaken the wolf inside her. But there wasn't one. And when it came down to it, she blamed me because she thought that I had stolen it all from her. It didn't matter that even if she was right in her thinking I wouldn't have been conscious of it as it would have happened in the womb, but she blamed me nonetheless and held my responsible for all the ills in her life." She sighed and tilted her head.

"The sad truth is that she could have had a life with us if she had been able to let go of her frustration. We would have allowed her to live with us and she could have been a wolf in spirit if not in actuality, but she couldn't accept that. Every time she saw one of us shift, she was consumed with jealousy and her heart only grew blacker. Then, one day, she left. I never thought I'd see her again. She thought that she would find the answers elsewhere, but she fell in with some bad people."

"Cyan," Alex said.

Her mother nodded. "That night...I could feel something happening in the wind, but I didn't listen to my instinct. Then they came, swarming around us like flies," she began to curl her hair more intently and her voice became more harrowed. "We tried to fight, but they were too powerful. I told you to run," her eyes flashed up at Alex.

"I wasn't quick enough. But they didn't keep me in Black Gate. They gave me to a man, taught me to fight. I'm still not sure why."

"Because she wanted to test you. This is all one of Sophie's great experiments," his mother said darkly. "She wanted to make you a creature of rage, to see if that would make any difference. She experimented on the others too. The only one she said she was going to keep alive was me, because she wanted to see me suffer. That's another reason why she separated us. She said that she wanted to know what it was like to be separated from the wolf, as though she knew what it was like to be separated from a child," there was a dry, cracked laugh that broke free of her mouth.

"I tried to rescue the others, but there wasn't enough time."

"There aren't as many left as there was. Sophie pushed so many of them to a breaking point," his mother shook her head. "Including your father…"

A moment of silence passed between the two of them.

"What are we going to do about her? She can't be allowed to get away with this."

"I don't know. What can we do? She's twisted and bent on revenge. I don't think there's anything that's going to stop her from finishing what she started."

"I hope there is because there's something else that's happened," Alex said. His mother flashed him a questioning glance. "I…became involved with a man,

Ben. This is his apartment. He helped me come to terms with who I am. He made me see that I'm not just a monster. And he's pregnant with my child."

His mother gasped and then smiled. "The wolf always finds a way. The spirit must be passed on," she said happily.

"But how is this possible?"

"There are forces at work that even science cannot understand. Our blood, it is the same, but different. The moon has its own will and we can only obey, but this is troubling. If Sophie knows this, she will try to use it to her own end. But I don't know what to do. Sometimes I wish there was something I could have done when we were children; something I could have said, or some way I could have convinced her that hatred was not the way to move forward. But she was deaf to everything."

"It wasn't your fault Mom. None of this could have been your fault. It's all on her, and we'll have to make her pay," Alex said. A weak smile flickered on his mother's face. She clasped her hands and trembled, nodding softly. A bird cawed outside, and it made her flinch. He worried about her tremendously as she had been through so much, and although she was looking much better than she had been, the road to recovery would be a long one.

"Mom, is there anything else you can tell me about what happened? Anything that might help?"

She thought for a moment, and then shook her head. "No, no I don't think so. I'm sorry. There is something you should think about Alex," she said. Alex arched his eyebrows. "You should think about running. Take this man you love and your child and get as far away from here as possible. Take them to the ends of the earth if you have to, if only to ensure that Sophie will never find you. I wouldn't put it past her to follow you until she takes her last breath, but you must make it difficult for her. She will do unspeakable things to get to you and your child. I dread to think what she's capable of after being so filled with rage and hatred all these years...it was bad enough that she could do all of this to her sister..." his mother's voice trailed off.

"I'll think about it Mom," Alex said, but in his heart, he knew he couldn't leave. Not when there were still wolves that were in danger. He was a fighter and he was going to fight for the people he loved for his pack. The more memories that came flooding back, the more he remembered how much they had meant to him and how he couldn't leave them. It was already frustrating that he couldn't save them all.

"Mom, Sophie isn't going to be happy that I rescued you and Ben, is she?" he asked. She shook her head. "Do you think that she'll take her anger out on the other wolves?"

His mother didn't reply, but the expression on her face told him everything he needed to know. His heart sank. He had spent all this time believing that he was a monster just because he was a wolf, when really it was Sophie. She was a full-blooded human, but she was more of a monster than he could ever be.

"She's taken so much from us already," his mom said, reaching out to clasp his hand. As she did so more memories came flooding back, memories of them running through the woods together. A smile flickered upon his face and he stood up.

"She hasn't taken everything though, and we've taken plenty back. Do you want to get out of here?" he asked. She understood the meaning behind his words. They walked out of the apartment and ventured to a thick forest nearby. Once they were certain they were out of sight of other people they shifted into wolves and yelped at each other. They bounded with each other and Alex was happier than he had been in a long time. His mom playfully snapped at him, and he dodged by jumping out of the way. Then, his mom sprinted away, flexing her limbs. Alex gave hot pursuit, but his mom seemed to be making up for lost time. She was incredibly swift and looked like a blur. Alex's tongue lolled out of his mouth as branches whipped against him. They ran over a river. Alex's hind leg caught the water and flecks of it burst up, before settling back on the river in a fine spray. For a moment he caught his reflection in the water, and he was filled with a profound sense of awe. This was him at his best, free and majestic, the way Ben saw him. The way he had always been meant to be.

What he was had been perverted and twisted by Hammond, forged into a weapon. Alex knew he was more than that now, as was his mother. She looked beautiful and ethereal as she ran through the wild, free from being caged, free from the trauma of being kept from her son and her pack. But as magnificent as this feeling was, it was also tinged with a bittersweet feeling as he knew that other wolves were being deprived of this feeling. They were still being held. It wasn't right. It wasn't just. Whatever Sophie was looking for, she wouldn't find it in them, but instead of releasing them she was keeping them caged up for her own amusement.

The happiness vanished from his heart and it was replaced by a haunting anger. He made a silent vow in that moment to make Sophie pay for everything she had done. There was much he didn't understand about the world, but he was beginning to trust his instincts, and they told him that Sophie and Cyan had to be stopped, no matter what the cost.

Chapter Four

Ben sat down in William's office, feeling as though he was in front of a school principal having broken some rules. Amelia was beside him, hands pressed in between her thighs. William shut the door behind them and settled into his chair, sighing loudly as he did so. He leaned back and formed a steeple with his hands, gazing towards the ceiling.

"My two intrepid reporters," he began. "Do you mind explaining to me why I just had a visit from two very intimidating people asking about you? Apparently, you ruffled a few feathers. They made some very interesting notions about lawsuits and veiled threats, asking how much this place would be worth. It almost seemed as though they were going to end up putting in a bid for the entire building. So, I'll ask again, what did you do?"

Ben and Amelia looked at each other surreptitiously again, so William continued.

"The last thing I told you was to be discreet and look into this matter. I told you to be careful because you're playing with fire. I've tried to protect you as best I could, but there's only so much I can do. How bad is this? How likely is Cyan to come down on us like a ton of bricks? Do I need to start warning people to look for new jobs?" he glared expectantly at Ben.

"It's worse than we feared. They kidnapped me William. They've kidnapped the other wolves as well. They're doing experiments. God knows what else they're doing. There's some scientist who is behind it all. She works at a place called Black Gate. It's a secret facility in the woods. That's where they're keeping all this, trying to hide it in plain sight."

"And what are these experiments trying to accomplish?" William asked.

"I don't know exactly. They're playing around with DNA, trying to manipulate genetics. I think they want to harvest werewolf genes for themselves."

Ben spoke hurriedly, the words pouring out of his mouth as he recounted everything that had happened, although he left out the worst parts of the torture, the parts that most anguished him.

"I see," William said in a deadpan tone. He cleared his throat and leaned forward, resting his elbows on his desk. "And do you have any evidence of this? Pictures? Reports? Witnesses?"

"It was kind of hard to get pictures while I was tied up," Ben said dryly.

"It's all there. I promise. Everything he said is true," Amelia said.

"Except we can't prove it, can we? And with a story like this we need cold, hard proof that nobody can deny. All this talk about the werewolves is going to make everyone dismiss it. Frankly, I'm still not sure if I believe it myself. Part of me wonders if the two of you have lost your minds and it's my faith in you that's being carried along for the ride. We need evidence. A company like Cyan isn't just going to roll over and let us say whatever we want to say. If we start printing stuff like this they're going to bury us in libel cases, and if we can't give any proof that this happened, and I'm sorry Ben and Amelia, but your experiences don't count as proof, then we're just going to end up being bankrupted by lawsuits. So, what can you give me? Believe me, I want to bury these guys as much as you, but I have to think about the bigger picture. We can't just go around shooting from the hip and making wild accusations. We have to build the evidence and make people see the truth. If we write about werewolves and secret experiments and mad scientists, they're just going to dismiss us as some fantasy magazine. I am not going to lose my reputation on this," he said.

Ben had a sinking feeling. "It's not fair," he said, and he began to choke on his emotion. "They kidnapped me William. They took me, tied me up, and threatened me. I don't know what would have happened to me if I hadn't been rescued. They need to be punished. They need to be stopped," he pleaded.

"You can't take us off this story William," Amelia added. "We're in too deep now. There have to be consequences for what they're doing. People have to know what's going on right under their noses. Cyan think they can hide all of this and nobody will bat an eye, but we have to show them they're wrong."

"So, show them!" William yelled, more strongly than either Amelia or Ben was prepared for. "Find the evidence. Get people who are willing to speak out against them. Cyan has covered its tracks well, but they must have made a mistake somewhere. Find me the sources that can back up what you're telling me. Let's write this story and give them no room to wriggle out of it. When we nail them, I want to make sure they can't escape." His words hung in the air for a few moments. "Well, what are you waiting for?"

Ben and Amelia didn't need any more encouragement than that. They left the office and discussed their next move.

"How are we going to get the evidence?" Ben asked. "We can't exactly go back to Black Gate and ask them to let us in and take pictures."

"No, but we have the financial records. That's something at least. It points to something shady going on. If we can just get a couple of people to speak out-"

Ben scoffed. "Nobody is going to be stupid enough to speak up against Cyan. They've all been paid off, and if anyone dares to think about what's going to happen, they know they're going to be punished. Cyan doesn't leave loose ends."

"I don't know, I think there might be more hope than you think. When Alex and I went to see Dr. Monroe she seemed filled with regret. She helped us once Ben, she might help us again."

"I don't know...she didn't seem very helpful when I saw her. And she didn't seem to regret anything either."

"She did in front of Alex. She felt sorry for him and she actually apologized. I think if we pushed her and worked on her she might budge, if we could get someone else as well. Maybe that's the key. Maybe we don't need just one person to blow the whistle, we need a whole group."

"Talk about asking for the impossible," Ben rolled his eyes. But then he sighed. "I might know one other person that could talk," he said. His tone was as cold as ice. "Hammond."

"Hammond?"

"It'll take some doing," Ben nodded, "but he's a bully, and bullies are cowards. I'm confident we could give him the right incentive to change his tack and talk to us about the work he did for Cyan. They trusted him with secrets, but we can break him open. I'll just need Alex's help."

"If you say so. I'll keep on looking at the financials and I'll try and dig up anyone else who might be willing to speak against them. I'll stay in contact with you. I'll send you a message at three o'clock every day. If I don't, then you know that I'm in trouble."

They bid farewell and went their separate ways. Ben returned home, trying to ignore the paranoia that crawled across his skin. He was relieved when he walked inside, although he was surprised that Alex and his mother weren't home. He was a little worried and his mind drifted to the worst outcome. What if Cyan had been here? But no...he dismissed that possibility quickly. If they had, then the place would have been far more of a mess. Thankfully it wasn't long before Alex and his mother returned. They seemed in good spirits, and Ben was pleased to see that Alex's mom was making progress.

Chapter Five

"Mom, this is Ben, Ben, this is my mother, Anne," Alex said, introducing her proudly. Anne smiled and took Ben's hand. He noticed the slight tremor, and the way she curled her hair and chewed on her bottom lip. These were all signs he recognized of great anxiety and stress. He picked at his nails and was amazed at how well Anne was holding up considering she had endured so many years of torture. The time he had spent at the mercy of Dr. Malone was bad enough, but years? It must have been her werewolf fortitude that had helped her survive. He had no doubt that he wouldn't have been able to last as long.

"It's a pleasure to meet you. Alex has told me that you have been a great help in his journey to rediscover himself. I thank you for that, and I feel as though I must apologize for my sister's actions as well."

"It's okay. I know that we can't always choose who we're related to," Ben smirked. "The truth is that Alex has helped me learn plenty about myself too. Did you tell her about...?"

Alex nodded.

"I was wondering if you could shed some more light on what happened. How is this possible? Will the baby be safe? Will I?" Ben's voice quaked as he spoke.

"You're going to be fine," Anne said in a reassuring tone. "I know it is highly unusual for you, but in wolf culture it is not uncommon. Your body will adjust, and when the time comes the baby will be lifted from you and all will be well."

"As long as Sophie doesn't interfere," Alex said bitterly.

"Anne, if the chance comes for you to testify about what happened to you, would you speak? Would you put your experience down on the record? Ben asked.

Anne drew into herself and looked unsure. "I do not know...to speak of what happened means speaking of our ways. We have always tried to maintain our privacy and keep our ways to ourselves. There are many who covet what we want, as you can see by Sophie's actions. I feel as though by revealing ourselves we might bring more attention onto us, and more danger into our lives."

"There's already plenty of danger," Alex said, a little harshly. Ben noticed the tension beginning to rise, so he acted quickly before an argument could break out.

"But if there was a way you could remain anonymous, or perhaps if you could talk about how you were kidnapped, but not why?"

"I think that would be more agreeable," Anne said. "But who would I be talking to, and why?"

"I'm a journalist and I want to bring Cyan down. I got into all of this when I was investigating the man who held Alex captive, Hammond. When we investigated him, we thought we had him dead to rights, until Cyan sprung some fancy lawyers and protected him. We found out that he had been receiving payments from Cyan, payments that began not long after Alex started fighting for Hammond.

They're in this together and if we can get testimonies against them it's going to be more difficult for them to deny that all of this happened."

Alex listened quietly. He didn't like how his mother would put the secrecy of the wolves over getting revenge on Cyan for all they had done, but he didn't want to get into an argument with her. Ben's idea sounded good, but it was flawed. Nobody was going to speak up against Cyan.

"Who else are you planning to call up? Are there people I don't know about?" Alex asked.

"Actually, I'm going to need you to help on this," Ben said. "Amelia and I were talking and we were thinking that you might be able to talk to Dr. Monroe. She seemed to have some affinity towards you." As he mentioned her name, Anne nodded.

"Julia tried to rein Sophie in, but she couldn't. Things got worse after she left," Anne said.

"I can try I suppose," Alex muttered.

"And then there's Hammond. I think we can get him to flip. If we can get to him then we can blow a huge hole in Cyan."

"I want to go to him," Alex said without a second thought. "You can talk to Julia. Take Mom with you, maybe it'll help Julia remember all the bad things she's done. Play on her guilt. I want Hammond for myself. I'll make sure he understands that he has no choice in the matter." Alex's heart leaped with the idea of getting a measure of revenge on Hammond.

Moving against Cyan was impossible at the moment, but Hammond? That was something Alex could do.

"Are you sure about this? I don't want anything happening to you."

"Nothing is going to happen to me. I promise. Hammond had been in chains before. He's not going to do the same again. You two work on Julia. And be careful with her. I don't think she'll take you again, not now she knows who you are. I don't think she'd want to risk harming the child either, if she does threaten you. Just take care of each other," Alex said. Ben and Anne nodded. They put together a timeframe; they would act when evening drew in because there was no time to waste. Ben called Amelia and told her the plan. She expressed her concern, but there was no stopping it no it was in motion. They were going to war with Cyan, and it was time to recruit some allies.

Chapter Six

Ben and Anne approached Julia's house. An unsettling feeling turned in his stomach, and he wasn't sure if it was the baby or his nerves.

"It's been so long since I've been out here," Anne said as she gazed out of the window and looked at the sights of the city. "I had begun to forget how beautiful it could be."

"I'm sorry you had to spend so long in Black Gate. I wish that things could have been different. It's not right what they did. We're going to make them pay, no matter how long it takes."

"I hope you do. When I think about that night and all the nights that have happened since…I'm only glad that Alex is well. There were so many times when I worried that he had been killed. I knew there were no depths that Sophie would not plunge to. I prayed that he was safe. Even though he had to go through a great ordeal himself I'm glad that he was able to come out the other side. I owe you a great debt Ben. You saved my son."

"Like I said, he saved me as well," Ben said.

Anne smiled. She seemed more at ease now than she had been when she was first rescued. Ben pulled up outside Julia's house and hesitated before he got out of the car.

"Is something wrong?" Anne asked.

"It's just that the last time I was here I was poisoned and then taken to Black Gate. I'm not quite sure this was the best idea. If Julia doesn't listen to us…"

"She'll listen. I'll make her," Anne said. There was a surprising amount of resoluteness in her voice, and Ben started to understand where Alex got some of his strength from. Ben quelled the anxiety inside and walked up to her house. Anne followed closely behind, gazing at the beautiful flowers all around them. When Julia answered the door, Anne was busy inspecting one of the flower beds, so it was only Ben who was standing in the doorway. Julia clutched the door and stiffened.

"I didn't expect to see you here again," she said, pressing herself up against the door as if to use it as a shield.

"No, I don't suppose you did. But thank you for telling me all about the history of Cyan. It shed a great deal of light on everything that was going on. I believe you met Alex," he said.

"I did, an intriguing young man," she replied. At this point Anne stood up and faced Julia. As soon as she did, all the color drained from Julia's face and she staggered back.

"Sophie…what are you doing here? I didn't…I didn't say anything. I promise. I don't know what he told you but I didn't betray you. I'm just minding my own business, like I always said I would. I've honored the agreement we made, I promise," she said, her words imbued with so much fear. Ben enjoyed watching her squirm. The feeling of being paralyzed in front of her was still fresh, the helpless feeling of having control of his body stolen from him. It was something he would never forget.

"I think we had better come in Dr. Monroe," he said. She stepped aside and let them in, closing the door behind them. It was only then that Ben revealed the truth.

"I take it you're afraid of Sophie?" he asked.

"Afraid would be a strong word, but I know what she's capable of and I'm not willing to push her to her limits," she said.

"Then you'll be glad to know that this isn't Sophie. It's Anne, one of the wolves she captured. Alex's mother."

"Anne..." Julia looked confused for a moment, then she was angry, and then she just seemed defeated. She sank down on a seat and leaned her head against her hand, sighing. "What do you want?"

"We want you to do the decent thing and speak out against Cyan. We want you to put a stop to what she's doing. These aren't just wolves; they're people, and they're being held against her will. You poisoned me knowing that she would have me. You need to do the right thing and get this story out."

"I can't. They'd destroy me."

"If you were the only one then yes, they might. But we're going to get others. We're going to shine a light on Cyan and ensure that they get punished, Sophie especially. She's been getting away with this for too long."

Julia let out a long, dry laugh. "You won't be able to get to her. She's protected. I made my choice a long time ago. You might not agree with it, but that's the choice I made and I can't go back on it now."

"You helped Alex once. You told him what happened."

"Yes…but I can't do it again. I'm sorry."

"Not even for me?" Anne asked. "I remember you Julia. I remember how you were always trying to protect us."

"Yes…I even tried to get Alex out of the way. I tried to do all I could, but it wasn't enough. Sophie…she was relentless. She had her dreams and nothing was going to get in her way, not even me. I'm sorry I was too weak, but there's nothing I can do. If I speak out, they'll just make sure I'm taken care of before anything gets to light. There's no way to win against them. They're the ones who make the rules to the game, and we have to play it as best we can."

"I won't accept that. I can't. They only win if people of conscience choose to stand by and let them win. If you're not going to do it for the wolves who have already died or the ones who are held captive, then do it for the ones she might harm in the future. Do it for the ones who you can still protect. Sophie isn't going to stop with them, is she? Where is it going to stop Julia? When is it going to stop? It's not, unless you stand up and tell the truth."

Anne's words were powerful, weighed down with all the power of what she had endured. Ben remained silent, letting her speak. Julia chewed her lower lip and looked fretful. She glanced around at her plants, her home.

"I can't…" she said in a small voice. "I made a promise. I said that I would never betray them. I…I'm sorry, but I can't do what you ask."

"Tell me something Julia," Ben said, not feeling like paying her the proper respect of addressing her as a doctor. "Do you think Sophie has any limits with who she'd target? What if there was a child? A baby? Do you think she'd stop there?"

"I…I don't know."

"But I think you do Julia. I think you know exactly what Sophie would do. Can you honestly live with yourself if you let this happen? There's a child in danger Julia. My child. She's not going to stop until she does whatever she wants to do in her perverse mind. Have you ever even asked yourself if it's possible for her to succeed at what she wants? All this pain, all this suffering, is it actually worth it? Why have all these people been through so much for Sophie's selfish endeavor?"

"You can say a lot of things about her, but you can't say that she's selfish. She's doing this for humanity," Julia said in a low, terse tone, glaring at Ben and Anne. "She wants to spread this gift around, to improve the human condition. If she can manage to splice the wolf genes into normal human DNA it will make us stronger, faster, it will make people able to withstand injuries and illnesses. We can improve people's lives."

"She's not interested in anyone but herself," Anne said bitterly. "If you think otherwise then you're deluding yourself. She only wants to make herself better, anything else is a lie."

Julia didn't respond, which told Ben that she knew Anne was speaking the truth.

"That may well be true, but it's still not as easy as you think. You don't know Cyan like I do. You don't know Sophie like I do. If they learn that I'm going to speak out against them they're going to stop anything from getting out. They value their privacy and they're not going to let someone like me ruin anything for them. They'll get to me."

"It's not just going to be you," Ben said, hoping that this wasn't going to be a lie. If Alex failed with Hammond, then Julia was going to be the only one. "We're going to work on getting more people, and Cyan can't deal with them all. The more people that speak out the more suspicious it's going to be if they start disappearing. All we need is a few brave people to come out first and lead the way. That's you Julia. You said that you know Cyan better than anyone, so you must know that what they're doing isn't right. You told Alex that you regretted what you did. I know you just want to be left alone here with your plants, but you don't have that luxury. There are people who need you," Ben spoke passionately. Julia looked dazed. The color had drained from her face. She rose from where she was sitting and walked over to one of her plants. The red rose and the wide leaves drooped down, as though they were weeping. She pinched them and ran her thumb across the surface of the leaf.

"All I wanted was to bring together humanity and nature. I thought by blending the two worlds I could make a better place. I didn't want to harm anyone. I didn't want to hurt anyone. I knew that Cyan wasn't exactly an ideal company to work for, but I thought I could use their resources to make the world a better place. Sophie thought so too...I knew her methods were more intense than mine. She kept pushing it harder and harder and by the end there wasn't anything I could do." Her head dropped. "I know it's wrong. I'm sorry for everything that's happened to you...if you can get more people to speak up then I'll think about it. I know you probably think I'm a coward, but we're all just trying to take care of ourselves in this world." She inhaled sharply and turned. "I will consider your proposal, but I cannot promise anything. Leave me your details and I will be in touch."

She spoke in such a way that indicated the meeting had run its course. Ben pulled out a card and placed it on the counter. He and Anne turned to leave, but before they did so he wanted to say one last thing.

"I think you might have been sticking around plants for too long Julia. You have to remember how people feel. You're not in this world alone. You can help people, people who aren't in a position to help themselves."

He didn't know if his words were going to have any effect or not, but he said them anyway. Julia didn't look at them as they left.

***

When Ben and Anne returned to the car, Ben slammed the door so fiercely the vehicle shook.

"Did that not go as well as you hoped?" Anne asked.

"No," Ben said tersely. "That damned woman has spent too much time with her plants. I wish I could talk some sense into her, but she seems to be in such willful denial it's impossible. How can she stand there knowing what she knows about Cyan and Sophie and do nothing? That's the problem, we're not just taking on Cyan, we're taking on everyone who won't speak out against them as well. Can't they see that as long as they don't say anything this is just going to continue? Nothing is going to change."

"She is right though. People tend to look out for themselves. Secrecy is a way of life for some. There are wolves over the years who have tried to urge us to reveal ourselves to the world, but we have always erred on the side of caution and kept ourselves hidden. I know it is not exactly the same situation, but I can see why she would want to keep herself safe. Not that it helps us."

Ben ran his hand across his scalp, frowning. "I really thought telling her that a child was in danger would make her change her mind, but she didn't even care."

"Perhaps she would have if the child was in front of her, but at the moment it remains within you," Anne said. Ben gulped. Talking about it was still such a strange thing.

"Has this happened often before? A human male becoming pregnant?"

"It is not unknown," Anne said. "I must admit that I am not entirely familiar with the situation myself, but you will be fine, as will the baby."

"I'm glad to hear you say it. I have to admit I'm still struggling with the concept of it all."

Anne smiled. There were moments like this when all the trauma of what she had been through slipped away and she was just a normal woman. "A child is always a blessing," she said. "I remember when Alex was born. The moon was full, it was a peaceful night. I looked down at him and I promised that I would give him the world. I wanted to make sure he had everything he could possibly want. I wanted his life to be filled with happiness. I couldn't fulfill that promise..." her voice trailed away and she sighed, gazing out of the window.

"It's not been as bad as you think. His memory came back eventually. I think he was just a little lost for a while there. But he is happy you're back. You were the first thing he remembered," Ben said. Anne smiled.

"I'm glad he had something like you to help guide him back to the truth. When I think of all he has been through...I just want him to be safe. When I think about that night I am so filled with pain. We should have done better. I knew that something was wrong. I could feel it in the air. I never thought Sophie would stoop so low as to come and attack the pack so brazenly. I thought that she might have had enough respect for us to let us live. But I was wrong. I thought too highly of my sister. I won't make the same mistake again."

"What do you think she's going to do next? She's not going to take kindly to us having escaped."

"No, she isn't. And she'll want to get you back, especially in your condition. You and Alex have naturally created what she's been trying to achieve all these years, a hybrid human and wolf. She'll want to learn its secrets, and she won't stop at anything," Anne's voice trembled.

"Is it even possible? Can Sophie actually do what she wants to do?"

"I do not know," Anne said wearily. "There was a time when I thought it would never be possible, but over the years I do wonder if science could reach a point where it could touch magic and reveal the things that have been hidden from us. Whether Sophie is the person to achieve that I do not know...she has been trying for so long without a result yet that I'm forced to wonder if it is at all possible. She is so determined, so zealous, that if it is possible, I would have thought she would have accomplished it already. But I don't think she's going to give up until she has exhausted every possibility. She has wanted this since birth. It is not something she can simply walk away from."

"That doesn't really bode well for the rest of us," Ben said dryly. He placed his hand on the ignition, ready to turn the key, but Anne said something that made him pause.

"I'm going to tell you the same thing I told Alex. You two should leave. You should get as far away from here and from Cyan as possible. Go somewhere you can be alone and raise your child in peace, without the threat of my sister coming after you. If you stay here she's never going to stop unless you actually succeed in what you are trying to do, but if everyone is like Julia then it's going to be difficult to get enough people to talk against Cyan. I know something about being involved in battles you can't win, and I'd hate for you and Alex to risk everything."

Ben listened to her, but he didn't reply. He started the engine and pulled away from Dr. Monroe's house with much on his mind. He had never walked away from a story before. He had always pursued the truth with a dogged determination, and he didn't have any intention of walking away from this story. And yet part of her wondered if there was sense to Anne's words. He was going to have a child. He couldn't just think of himself any longer. He had to consider the child. Already it was changing his thinking and making him less reckless, but then he wondered if he was just as bad as Julia. If he gave up the story now, who would continue battling against the horrors that went on at the behest of Cyan?

That was if they even had a story of course. Julia was unwilling to talk, so he hoped that Alex had better luck with Hammond.

Chapter Seven

Alex's hands were clenched into tight, knotted fists that were held rigidly by his side as he made his way to Hammond's bar. For a long time it had been the only place that was known to him. His memory had been stolen from him, and he had been prevented from helping his pack. He'd trained as a fighter and been forced to defeat opponents at Hammond's behest. It felt good to act under his own will again, to move forward with a purpose and with a sense of resolve in his heart. He snarled as he approached, all the festering hatred burning inside him. He walked up to the door and pushed right through the bouncer, who cursed at him.

People had trickled into the bar. All of the eyes were on a danced who gracefully moved around the stage, clinging to the pole as though it was the only thing giving her life. Emma came up to him and smiled.

"Haven't seen you since you rushed out of here," she said. "Everything alright? How was that date of yours?" she said with a friendly smile.

"It was fine," Alex said.

"Mr. Hammond wants to see you. I think he's been worried."

"I'm sure he has," Alex didn't stop his stride and continued moving forward, marching away from her. Emma arched her eyebrows and shook her head, not pursuing him. Alex made his way to Hammond's office and burst through the door. It closed automatically behind him. Hammond was sitting behind his desk, and he rose when he saw Alex.

"Alex! My boy! I've been so worried about you! I thought I told you never to leave without telling me where you're going? It's a dangerous world out there and I'd hate for anything to happen to you. There are so many things that just aren't right and I wouldn't be able to live with myself if you got into trouble. Please, come, sit down and let's talk. Now, I know you've been a little unhappy with the way things have progressed. You want more out of life than fighting and I understand that, I truly do. First, I have to apologize to you. I think I got caught up in the excitement of it all, you know, it's rare to find someone like you Alex, someone who is so good at what he does. But if you want a change then we can make a change. You won't have to fight anymore, I promise. There are plenty of other ways to make money and I'm sure we'll find a profitable endeavor."

He spoke quickly, not giving any chance for Alex to respond, but Alex didn't mind this. Let Hammond talk, he always liked talking too much, and soon enough he would start saying something that Alex wanted to hear. Alex stood there seething with his arms crossed against his broad chest.

"There have to be plenty of things you're good at," Hammond continued. "But as it happens, I do have a few connections in the city. One of them is actually looking for someone at the moment. I'm not entirely sure what the role is, but I have no doubt that you'd be well suited for it. Perhaps I could arrange a meeting and you could start becoming more than a fighter? That's something you really want, isn't it?" he said.

Alex sniffed the air. Hammond smelled of desperation. Alex turned up his nose and sighed heavily.

"Actually, I've decided that I'm happy being a fighter," Alex said, "it's just that now I'm going to be fighting for a cause I believe in."

"Oh?" Hammond asked, feigning curiosity. "And what cause would that be exactly?"

Alex smirked and made his way around the desk. His aura was big enough to feel the room. Up until this moment he had always cowered before Hammond. Hammond had been the one with the power, and Alex was the one unsure of himself. But that had all changed now and it was Hammond who backed away, pressing himself against the wall. Alex towered over him, looming like a demon.

"The one where I take down Cyan," he said. There was a flicker of recognition in Hammond's eyes, although he tried to deny anything.

"Cyan? That big company? Why would you want to take them down?" he asked.

"Don't play dumb with me Hammond. I know that you're in bed with them. I know what you've done. I know how you got me. And you're the one that's going to help me take them down."

"What? No! I...I know nothing," he said, panicked. Alex smirked, a smirk that quickly turned into a snarl. He bore down upon Hammond until there was nothing else in Hammond's vision, but for a moment Hammond showed resistance.

"Don't do this Alex. You know it's only going to cause trouble for you. If you know Cyan then you know that, and if you don't stop, I'm going to put you in chains again. I'm going to make sure to punish you like I punished you before. Do you remember what that was like Alex? Do you remember all the pain? All the anguish? Do you remember how you struggled? You don't want to go back to that again do you Alex? You can make sure you don't by stopping all this now. You can just leave this office and we'll pretend that this never happened. I won't hold it against you. I won't even try to stop you. You can leave, I promise," he said. Alex didn't believe him. He could smell the lies on Hammond's breath.

"Your confidence is misplaced if you think that you can scare me. You have no power anymore Hammond. No power at all," he said, and as Alex said this his face shimmered into that of a wolf, of the beast that Hammond had conjured inside him, had driven to fighting so much. When Hammond saw it, his face went as white as a sheet and he groaned hauntingly. He raised his hands in supplication and begged Alex not to hurt him.

"I'm not going to hurt you Hammond, as long as you tell me what I want to hear. But we're not going to do it here in your office where it's safe. We're going down to the pit," Alex said. Hammond's eyes widened in fear, but he wasn't in a position to negotiate.

***

Alex and Hammond walked through the bar, acting as though nothing was wrong. Alex had warned Hammond that if he tried to raise the alarm, Alex would tear the bar apart. Hammond had seen what Alex could do in battle, so he knew the man wasn't bluffing. Alex was only annoyed that he had let this man control his destiny to such an extent, and he felt ashamed that he had let this man get away with so much. It showed him that strength was not just a matter of muscles, but it was an attitude as well, and Alex vowed that he would never be weak again.

They went down into the fighting pits, a huge arena that was built into the basement underneath the bar. The air was dusty and sand was all over the ground. When it was empty like this it felt eerie and surreal, as though it didn't belong here at all. Around the fighting pit there were chains. During an event these chains were linked to form a barrier, helping to keep the crowds from rushing in and interfering, but when they weren't being used for that they had another purpose, one that Alex knew all too well. As soon as he saw them he rubbed his wrists, and bitter anger flared within him. He pointed to them and told Hammond to go over there.

"No, Alex, come on, you don't need to do this. We can just talk like two people," he said, his eyes widening with panic when he saw the chains. But Alex was determined in his resolve.

"You didn't talk to me like a person when you had me here. You had me in chains as you taught me how to be a fighter. You lashed me and treated me like a beast, hoping that that was what I would become. Well, maybe you succeeded. And maybe I want to see what you'll turn into," he said. He took hold of Hammond's collar and dragged him towards the chains. Hammond's feet kicked out against the ground, but Alex's strength was too much for him to resist against. Alex threw him to the ground and Hammond went sprawling. A thin layer of dust rose as he crashed to the ground, and he scrambled against the wall, which was exactly where Alex wanted him.

Alex took the chains and wrapped them around Hammond's wrists and ankles, looping them around to form a metal knot. The chain was cold and heavy in his hands, as was his heart at the memory of how he had suffered because of them. Pain flared in his mind as he thought of Hammond barking orders at him, whipping him with chains as he was forced to shift even when he didn't want to, as he was forced to fight. Hammond's pleas were incessant, but Alex blocked them from his mind. He was here for one thing and one thing only, and nothing was going to stop him from that.

Once Hammond was tied up in chains, Alex stood over him, towering like the Colossus of Rhodes. Hammond was shaking and his eyes glistened with tears. Such a powerful man looked pathetic in chains, and Alex was filled with nothing but disgust for him.

"What do you want from me Alex? I don't know anything. I promise. I'm not as important as you think I am. I'm just a cog in a machine. I don't mean anything. I have this bar and that's it."

"Except that's not true, is it? You worked with Cyan. They gave me to you and you turned me into this beast. You knew everything that was happening and they paid you for it. Why? Why did they want me? Why did you do this to me?" he asked. Hammond continued to deny everything and shook his head, which just drove Alex insane with anger.

He closed the short distance between them and grabbed a fistful of Hammond's hair, pulling it so tightly that Hammond's neck twisted back and pain rippled across his face. He gasped.

"Don't test me Hammond. You're not in control here any longer. I am. I spent too long at your heel, not asking why you were doing this. I know you know more than you're letting on and I'm not going to stop until you tell me the truth. I already have you in chains. You can always tell me now, or you can make me angry. And you know what happens when you make me angry. You wanted a beast didn't you Hammond? You trained me to be full of hate and rage. Maybe that's what you want now. Maybe that's the only way I can get anything out of you," Alex said. He stepped back and stretched his arms out like wings, lifting his gaze to the ceiling as he summoned the primal energy within him. It swirled and pulsed in a hot burst, and he could feel the relief. His nails sharpened into claws and his face took on the visage of a beast. A low growled rumbled out of him, its intent as furious as a storm.

Before the transformation could be completed, Hammond wailed and shook his head, surrendering under the threat of being at the mercy of his creation.

Alex breathed deeply and calmed his beating heart, returning to his human form.

"I'm glad you're seeing sense. Now, why don't you tell me exactly what's going on? How did you come to work for Cyan?"

"I've…I've done some odd jobs for them over the years, you know, covered a few things up, held some products for them, nothing serious. Then I got a message from someone who worked there. She said she needed someone discreet and she offered me more money than I'd ever seen before. Hell, for that amount I would have been discreet about anything. It was a strange plan though. There were two of them. Two doctors. One of them told me that the other was going to approach me to take a man away, someone who had been experimented on. Apparently it was a failed experiment. All I had to do was say yes and take you with me, and then report back to the first doctor, who knew everything that was happening. She said that she wasn't ready for the experiment to end yet, that she wanted to learn more, and she could only learn it in an environment that wasn't a laboratory."

"What kind of experiment? What did she want to learn about me?" Alex said. When Hammond faltered and failed to answer straight away, Alex yanked one of the chains. Hammond's arm shot out and he gasped in pain. His shoulders slumped and he looked much the worse for wear.

"She…she said that she wanted to learn how much was in your nature. She wanted to know your potential if you were truly angered. She gave you a drug to suppress your memory and then she gave you to me. She told me to give you nothing but a violent life. The other doctor thought that you would have been safer with me than in the laboratory, but she was wrong. You were exactly where the other one wanted you to be. I sent her reports of your progress, of what I observed. I don't...I don't know what she wanted to learn in the end. I just know that she was interested to see how you would react."

"Well, now she knows," Alex replied grimly. He took a moment to process everything that Hammond was telling him, a moment that Hammond was grateful for as it allowed him to catch his breath and brace himself against the pain. Alex paced around in front of Hammond.

"What does she want now? When was the last time you spoke to her?" he asked. When Hammond took longer to answer than Alex wanted, Alex yanked a chain again, and Hammond howled in pain. It still wasn't anything compared to the treatment that Alex had been subjected too. The chains had bitten into his skin and were used as whips against his thick hide when he was in his beast form. If he whipped Hammond, he would at least tear skin away, if not leave Hammond with broken bones and perhaps even close to death. Alex wasn't at that point yet.

"Tell me!" he yelled.

"She wants me to bring you to her! She said she's not done with you." Hammond let out a low laugh, although it was devoid of humor. "You really are a fool if you think you can take Cyan on and come out unscathed. I saw the results of what you did. I always knew that you could fight anyone Alex but taking on Cyan is a different matter entirely. You should quit while you're ahead. We both should."

"Oh, I'm not ready to quit yet, and neither are you. You're going to help me take down Cyan."

Hammond stared at Alex in disbelief. "I'm what?"

"You heard me. They're not going to get away with what they've done, and you're not going to get away with it either. It's time for you to do something noble with your life Hammond, to make up for the mistakes you've made. You're going to talk about your work with them and everything they've done. All the dodgy deals, all the crimes; it's all going to come out in the light, and it's all thanks to you."

"No...Alex...you can't expect me to do that! Do you think I have a death wish? If I start saying that Cyan are going to come after me. They're going to kill me. Do you think anyone is going to miss me? Nobody is going to care to investigate."

"I'm sure your wife would."

Hammond spat. "I know she hates me. Do you think I'm blind? This bar, this little piece of the world is all I have. Please Alex, if I start speaking out against Cyan, they're going to take everything away from me."

"Just like they tried to take everything from me," Alex said pointedly. "But I got my memory back Hammond, and I'm not going to let them get away with this. You're going to talk. Because if you don't Cyan are going to be the last thing you have to worry about." He moved close to Hammond and leaned down, so close that Hammond could feel the warm caress of his breath. "I learned a lot while I was here, and I remember all those lessons too. If you don't do exactly as I say, then I'm going to put into practice all that I learned from you. I'll tear you limb from limb and I'll leave you as wrecked as all the people I fought for you. There won't be a place on your body that doesn't hurt," Alex hissed.

Hammond gulped. As it to punctuate his point Alex took hold of Hammonds forearm and squeezed, digging his nails into the flesh.

"Okay, okay, I'll do it. I'll do what you ask," he said. "Just please, get me out of these chains."

"You know I'll be watching you Hammond. I'm taking your word on this. If you try to do anything that goes against this, you're going to be sorry. My friend will be in touch and you can go on the record with everything you've learned. Think of this as turning over a new leaf. You can start to make up for all the mistakes you made," Alex said. He pulled away one of the chains, but let Hammond take away the rest.

***

Alex marched back up the stairs and returned to the bar. He made his way to Emma and spoke to her in a low voice.

"I need you to do me a favor Emma. Don't ask why, just please trust that I need you to do this. I want you to keep a close eye on Hammond. If he goes anywhere or has any unusual meetings, I want to know about it. Don't let him out of your sight. This is as important as life or death," he said. Emma nodded, although she had a confused look in her eyes.

Chapter Eight

Ben was waiting for Alex to return. Anne had gone out to enjoy the fresh air and to run free through the forest. Ben had reminded her to be careful, but he knew that she would be. She wouldn't risk being captured again. When Alex returned Ben leaped up and hugged him tightly, before leading him back to the sofa. Alex was taut with tension and he glowered, although his expression lightened when he was reunited with Ben.

"How did you get on with Julia?" Alex asked.

Ben sighed. "Not as well as I hoped. She doesn't seem willing to help at all. She's convinced that Cyan is going to get here and she's not willing to take the risk. I think you overestimated her sympathy for you."

"Yes, well, I learned that not everything is as it seemed. Julia told me that she felt sympathy for me, but it was Sophie who was behind everything. She knew what Julia was doing. She's been in control this whole time. She suppressed my memory because she wanted to see what I would be like if I didn't know who I was. She treated me like some experiment, and she's not finished yet."

"Sounds like Hammond told you a lot," Ben said.

"He did, and he agreed to testify."

Ben arched his eyebrows in surprise. "That's great news!" he said. "I wasn't sure that Hammond would flip, but I guess we were right and he's just a coward at heart. Where is he now?"

"I left him at the bar."

"You what? Alex, do you think that's wise?"

"It's the only thing he has Ben. He's not going to leave it now. Besides, I have another plan."

"What do you mean?"

"Hammond said that he was going to work with me and talk about everything he knows, but I know him better than he thinks I do. We spent a lot of time together, and while he was training me, I was observing him. I spent a lot of time learning about the kind of man he was, and I know he's not just going to turn around and betray Cyan. They've paid him too much money, and he'll probably think that he can get them to protect him and maybe even pay him more if he tells them about me. As soon as he meets with them, I'm going to go, because I know that he's going to meet with Sophie. I'm going to talk with her and put an end to this all."

"It sounds risky," Ben said pensively, turning his head away as he didn't want Alex to see the doubt and hesitation in his eyes.

"It is, but it's less risky than invading Black Gate again. Getting to Sophie is the key here," he said.

"What if…what if we don't?"

"Well, if we don't get to Sophie then I don't know what else we plan to go. I guess I can go and talk to Julie, perhaps talk some sense into her. Maybe she knows someone else who might be willing to talk."

"No Alex, I mean what if we don't investigate Cyan anymore. What if we just walk away and leave the whole thing behind," Ben said. Alex stared at him as though he was speaking in another language. "I know this is important, but we have other things to think about now. Your mom spoke to me today and she said that we should get as far away from here as possible if we want a happy life. The more I think about it, the more I wonder if she's right. As much as I hate to admit it, the odds of beating Cyan are low, and if we don't win there's going to be a huge target painted on our back. I don't want to live my life in fear. I don't want to be worried that someone is always going to be chasing us. Maybe we should just let it go," Ben said. The words were bitter on his tongue, but they needed to be spoken.

Alex remained silent for a few moments. "I can't believe you would say such a thing. What about the truth? What about justice? What about all the wolves still locked up there?"

"What about our child?" Ben shot back. Hot tears stung his eyes as his words reverberated into silence. The tension between them was palpable. Ben leaned forward and placed his head in his hands. Alex was sitting with a straight back, staring into space. He spoke next, and his words were deliberate.

"I wouldn't want to have to explain to my child how I left people behind. I want to set an example for them. Running away…it doesn't solve anything. It just leaves it for someone else to deal with. I can't let that happen Alex. I'm sorry, but I can't be the kind of man who just walks away. I know what you and Mom are saying comes from a good place, but it's not the kind of man I am, and I don't think it's the kind of man you are either."

"If I'm being honest, I don't know what kind of man I am anymore," Ben said with a rueful smile. "I'm not sure how I'm supposed to be feeling or what I'm supposed to be doing. I just want this to be over so I can focus on having a baby."

"You're a good man Ben. You're the man I love," Alex said." You're the man who saved me." He placed his hand upon Ben's and smiled. Somehow that made all the difference in the world.

"I want this to be over too, but I want it to be over because we've done all we can. I don't want to leave anything behind. I don't want to stop this just because we're afraid of Cyan. They've been allowed to bully people for too long. They took my memory from me Ben. They took my mother. I don't want them to get away with this."

"I don't either," Ben said. "I'm just worried, that's all."

"It's okay to be worried. I am too. I just know that I won't be able to live with myself if I don't do anything."

"What are you going to do if Hammond does lead you to Sophie?"

"I don't know, but I'll figure something out. I'll talk to her, stop her anyway I have to. It seems as though she's the driving force behind this so if we stop her then it might stop the whole thing."

"I guess it should be doable. She's only human after all," Ben said, although his tone was grim because he knew that Sophie was a formidable enemy. He remembered the pure hatred that emanated from her, the cruelty and the malevolence. When he looked into her eyes, he saw nothing but a need to hurt people, and he had never been more afraid. He curled his arms around his body and gulped. "I don't want her to get her hands on either of us again."

"Neither do I. It won't happen. I promise," Alex said softly, cooing into Ben's ear. He wrapped his arm around Ben's shoulders and pulled him into him. Ben allowed him to do so, sinking into his comforting warmth and the love that was freely offered. Ben tilted his head up and smiled.

"You shouldn't make promises you can't keep," he said. Alex grinned and let his hand slide across Ben's body, resting on his stomach.

"I promise that I'm going to love you until the sun fades from the sky," he said, leaning down to plant a soft kiss upon Ben's lips.

"I'm going to love you until the stars fall," Ben replied. He shifted his body over so that he was sitting on Alex's lap. Wrapping his arms around Alex's shoulders, he tilted his head to the side and gave Alex a deep kiss, sinking into the warmth and the honeyed lust that was always present between the two of them. Alex's hand fell down to Ben's waist and then rested against his thigh, squeezing it as they kissed. Ben gasped a little, feeling the burning tension rising inside him, bursting out like a flaming breath.

Alex buried himself in Ben's neck, kissing and nibbling at his skin. Ben's breaths grew deeper and heavier as he tilted his neck back. His lips parted in anticipation. Alex's hand drove deeper in between his thighs, fondling the bulge that swelled there. Ben could feel Alex shifting underneath him. Ben playfully pulled off Alex's top, revealing the masculine body underneath. Arousal and desire flared within him at the sight of this man, the man that had claimed his heart and soul. Ben kissed along the collarbone and across his chest, while letting his hand run down the middle of Alex's torso, before resting against his crotch and the hard arousal that promised so much delight.

Alex pinched the hem of Ben's skirt and pulled it over his head, tossing it away. His hands wrapped around Ben's body and the feeling of his ardent fingers against exposed flesh brought exquisite delight to Ben's mind. They drowned in loving kisses, the heat rising between them. Alex started to fumble with Ben's belt and pants, so Ben slid himself off of Alex so that he too could escape the confines of his clothes. They laughed and grinned as they could barely keep their hands off each other. They kicked off their pants and the clothes landed in a puddle on the floor. Clad in only their boxers, Ben threw himself into Alex's arms. Their flesh pressed against each other as they lost themselves to a flurry of kisses. Their tongues swirled and danced as they pulled themselves off the couch and made their way to the bed, stumbling across the lounge as they couldn't bear to take their hands or their lips off each other.

When they got into the bedroom, they flung themselves on the bed and giggled as they pulled the covers over themselves. They ran their hands all over each other's bodies, and a wave of tingles was left behind. They shared kisses and breathed in the masculine musk that rose between them. A mischievous twinkle gleamed in Alex's eyes as he left a trail of kisses down Ben's body, stopping at his abdomen. He looked at it with ardor and they both thought about the life they were creating together. Alex smiled and kissed Ben's stomach lovingly, before he slipped his hand down and peeled away his underwear, revealing his burning arousal. Alex curled his hands around the shaft and moved his lips down, before Alex shuddered and groaned with pleasure. He let his arms splay out either side of him and closed his eyes, enjoying all the intense sensations as Alex pleasured him. Warm breath rippled over his thighs and he was soon in heaven as Alex slipped his warm lips down, taking him deeper and deeper into his mouth.

Ben's back arched as pleasure coursed through his body. Blood rushed through, flushing his skin with a deep crimson shade. One of his hands fell down and rested against Alex's head. Ben murmured with delight as he felt the gentle bobbing rhythm as Alex pleasured him, moving his head up and down, wet saliva dripping from his mouth. In the shadows of the blanket Alex looked beautiful, intimately connected with Ben. The pleasure became more intense and it felt as though a fire was being stoked in his soul. As Alex nestled in between his legs he could feel Alex's arousal pressing against him and he wanted it so bad, but he was left breathless by Alex's mouth and tongue, so much so that he couldn't make any noises apart from incoherent moans.

His head tilted from side to side against the pillow as the pleasure became almost too much for him to bear. He groaned loudly as sweat prickled upon his skin and tingled all over, as though electricity was crackling over his body. His mind grew hazy, intoxicated by lust, and his chest rose and fell with each heaving breath. Then, Alex drew himself up and continued to massage Ben's erection. He was so tall, and all the beautiful angles of his body were cast in a glorious light. It was as though he was radiant.

Alex took Ben's hand and brought it to his lips. He kissed the fingers and then opened his mouth, taking them deep inside, sucking on them as he had sucked on Ben's erection. Then, he drove it down his body, into the shadows where dark pleasures and intimate delights existed. Ben felt the heat as Alex guided his hand into the depths of him, feeling all the tight warmth. It made his own cock twitch as he felt his fingers submerging into the depths of the man he loved. Alex grinned and groaned as he let his head drop back. Breath rushed out of him and he shuddered, all at the behest of Ben's touch. Pleasure swam between them, making the air shimmer with erotic and sensual heat. Just one gentle curl was enough to make Alex wild with pleasure, and it soon became clear that he wanted more.

Ben was ready to give it to him.

Alex pulled Ben's hand away as he shifted his position to straddle Alex. He lowered himself onto Alex's erection, and both men moaned as their bodies came together. Ben's hands clasped his waist as Alex steadied himself. He licked his lips and smirked as he started to rock back and forth. Ben clamped his eyes shut and every muscle in his body went taut as Alex rocked on top of him. Alex leaned over and took control of the momentum. Sweat drizzled off his body and sizzled on Ben's burning skin. They kissed hard and fervently. Ben felt as though he was going to explode. Each moment took him close to that glorious release. His eyes swam with desire and love as he looked at Alex, gazing at the man who had captured all of him. They kissed wildly before Alex reared up again, and at the sight of him Ben knew he couldn't hold it in any longer. He gripped onto Alex so tightly that his fingers dug into Alex's skin. His hips moved like pistons. His body seemed to have a mind of its own, fueled by pure instinct, everything inside him devoted to one goal, one cause: the release of all his lust and love and passion.

It came driving through his body like a whirlwind, leaving nothing in its wake. Ben could feel the unstoppable, relentless force and he loved every second of it. Part of him wished that it would never end, but the real joy came with the climax. It surged through him and then his body shuddered violently as the ecstasy hit him. Terse breaths punched the air and sweat dripped from his brow. Soaked flesh slid against him as Alex pulled himself off and slid beside Ben, still hard.

Ben's hand slipped down. He was so dazed he felt as though he was dreaming, but he wanted Alex to feel as good as he did.

"Do you want to be inside me?" he whispered.

"I just want to be close to you. This is good,"
Alex said, kissing him, curling his arms around him as
he pressed himself as close to Ben as was possible.
Ben massaged, stroked, and squeezed, wanting to
bring him even just an echo of the sensations he had
felt. The strength had rushed out of his body, but he
managed to muster enough to pleasure Alex. Alex
murmured sweet things into Ben's ear, and his biceps
curled, displaying all of his masculine strength. It was
enough to make Ben swoon and within moments he
could feel the desire flooding out of Alex. The hot lust
drenched his skin and scorched him, but it was a
wonderful, delirious sensation. Their bodies stuck
together as they kissed, wrapping their legs together
like vines. Neither of them cared that they had made
themselves a mess. They were just happy to be
together, and if Ben had his way, they would never be
apart. He held onto Alex tightly and whispered a
promise to the man he loved. Alex made a vow back,
a secret that was kept between themselves. It was
something sacred and lasting, some beautiful and
wondrous, and it was all theirs.

Chapter Nine

After basking in the glow of their love, the two men rose when they heard Anne return. They cleaned themselves up and got dressed, although they looked sheepish when they had to pick their discarded clothes up off the floor of the lounge. Anne didn't seem to mind though.

"How was your run?" Alex asked. He was glad to see that his mother was becoming more like herself again.

"It was satisfying. There are still moments when I fear that someone is watching me, and running by myself is not exactly the same as running with the pack, but it is nice to feel the wind in my hair again and to breathe in the scents of nature."

"It won't be long before you're with the pack again Mom," Alex said. He meant it as a promise.

"Has something happened? Has progress been made?" she asked.

"Not exactly," Ben said, shooting a wary glance towards Alex. Alex explained to her everything that had happened with Hammond, and how he planned to ambush a meeting with Sophie. As soon as he mentioned this idea, a look of horror spread across Anne's face.

"No, you can't," she gasped. "You can't go anywhere near her. That's playing right into her hands. All she wants is to get her hands on you. If you do this, you'll be hers, and she'll do anything she wants with you. We've only just got each other back Alex. We can't lose each other so quickly."

"This is coming from the woman who wants us to run away? We're not leaving Mom. We can't afford to leave. We have to stop Sophie, and as soon as I get the opportunity, I'm going for it. I'm not going to wait and I'm not going to let the wolves suffer any longer than they need to."

"And how do you expect to get them out? Do you think Sophie is going to let you? She won't ever do what you want, no matter what you hold over her or threaten her with, and Cyan are hardly going to let her," Anne said harshly. Tension rose between them. Alex could feel his blood boiling. He hated to argue with his mother, but he didn't want anything to get in his way of his mission.

He was about to bite back, but Ben spoke first and defused the tension.

"Let's not fight between ourselves. That's no way to get to a corporation like Cyan. Come on, let's just try to keep our heads clear and relax. We all want the same thing; we just have to go about finding the right way to achieve it. Let me get Amelia over and we can talk about the different options we have. Agreed?"

Alex and Anne nodded. Alex breathed deeply and tried to calm himself down. There was so much tension around that he was starting to fight with the people he loved, but he couldn't let this get the better of him. He had spent so long fighting that he had to remember there were some people he didn't have to fight with. Thankfully Anne didn't want to argue any more either. She went to her room to rest, while Alex and Ben watched some TV, trying to take their minds off of things.

***

When Amelia arrived, Anne emerged from her room and they ordered a couple of pizzas to share. They all looked tired and gaunt, Amelia especially so, although she looked more relaxed now that she was in company.

"I tell you what, I hate living by myself when something like this is going on. Every damned noise that I hear I keep thinking that it's someone from Cyan coming to get me," she threw herself onto the couch in a huff. Ben quickly updated her on everything that had happened, and then asked if she had made any progress with her end of research.

"Unfortunately, no," she began. "Cyan knows how to weave a web alright. I mean, I can prove links to various companies, so I can prove that Cyan invested in Black Gate, but I can't prove what goes on there. We need testimonies. Whatever I can give up might sway people along with actual reports, but it's not enough on its own."

"Well, I struck out with Julia," Ben said.

"At least Hammond will talk," Alex said.

"Yeah, but he's only one man, and a criminal at that. He's hardly the most trustworthy of sources, and I doubt Cyan will have a difficult time discrediting him if he's the only person we can conjure up," Amelia said.

"Dammit," Ben curled his hand into a fist and hung his head.

"We have to go ahead with my plan. It's the only way," Alex said.

"What plan?" Amelia asked.

Anne sighed. "He thinks that Hammond is going to get in contact with someone at Cyan, possibly Sophie herself, and when he does, Alex wants to be there to confront her directly," Ben said, sounding more than a little irritated, although Alex didn't know if this was because he didn't like the idea, or if he was just angry with the situation as a whole.

"I'm not seeing a problem with that. Maybe that's what we have to do, go to the source," Amelia said. Alex smiled at her, glad that someone was on his side and saw the sense of the matter.

"The only problem is that's playing right into Sophie's hands. She wants us to find her and there's no telling what she's going to do. We can't risk it, and we don't even know if she's going to be alone," Ben said.

"But it's the only way to free the rest of the pack. I don't care who she brings with her. I can take them out. We need to speak with her," Alex said, his voice rising in anger again.

"But I ask you again, how are you going to get her to free them? Cyan aren't going to let you back into the facility, and there's not going to be anything you can say that would convince her," Anne said. Her question hung in the air and everyone remained silent for a few moments, everyone except Amelia.

"Aren't we missing the obvious here?" she asked, glancing at Anne. The others didn't seem to follow her train of thought, and Alex wondered what she was getting at.

"Well," she continued, "if we have to get into the facility to rescue the rest of the pack and the only way we'll get in with her is...well...to use her?" Amelia pointed towards Anne. "You did say they were twins, right? If we follow Hammond and we manage to capture Sophie, maybe we can dress Anne up as her and she can get into the facility, release the pack, and then we can focus on taking Cyan down. At least if they're freed, they're not going to suffer. Even if we manage to gather evidence against Cyan it's going to take a long time to see them punished, and the longer that takes, the more the prisoners are going to suffer."

It was a great solution and Alex was impressed. "That's perfect!" he said, but Anne was hesitant.

"I don't know...I can't do that. I can't be her," she said.

"Yes you can Mom. You're identical twins. If we get her clothes and her ID, you'll easily be able to pass for her. You can go in and release everyone and get out before anyone realizes something has gone wrong!"

"They'll know I'm not her. They'll realize I'm pretending and they'll capture me again. I can't go back there. I can't," she said, her voice quickening as she spoke, her anxiety growing. She started to rock back and forth on the couch. Amelia and Alex glanced at each other. Ben knelt on the floor and rested a hand on her shoulder.

"It's going to be okay Anne. I know that you don't want to go back in there, and I don't envy you, but you won't be alone. I'll go with you," he said.

"What?" Alex replied. Ben twisted his neck to look at him.

"It's okay. I know what your mom is going through. I don't want to go back there either, but we have to, for the pack. Amelia is right. I think we've been going about this the wrong way. Taking Cyan down is too big for us at the moment. We don't have the evidence. We need to think about the people that are still suffering at their hands. Anne, you can take me in, saying that you finally have what you need. We'll work on getting the prisoners freed. Once they are, we'll get out of there as quickly as possible, and then we'll deal with whatever Cyan chooses to hit us with. While you're freeing the prisoners, I'll try and find as much evidence as I can that will help our case. I'll get pictures and videos. We might actually stand a chance."

"No, I can't let you do that Ben. Not when you're carrying our child. It's too dangerous. I should be the one to go. I'm the wolf. I'm the fighter," Alex said.

"Which is why we're going to need you to make sure Sophie and Hammond don't escape. Besides, they know you're a threat and they'll probably sedate you or put you in chains. At least I'm just a human.

They know I won't do anything." Ben then looked to Anne. "Just be confident. We'll be together. We won't let anything happen to each other and as soon as we've freed the wolves we can leave immediately."

Anne breathed deeply and nodded. Alex was so proud of Ben in that moment and loved him for putting himself at risk. Alex knew that Ben had suffered greatly at the hands of his aunt, and to go back to Black Gate took great courage. Alex couldn't think of anyone he would rather have carrying his child.

"I'm happy to go ahead with this if everyone else is, but I want both of you to know that if anything happens to either of you I am running in there and tearing Black Gate down from the inside, I don't care what it costs. I'm not losing either of you," Alex said, and he was deadly serious.

"I wouldn't expect anything less," Ben said, grinning. Now that they had a plan the tension had been reduced. It felt better knowing that they had a way forward through this mess, and that the other wolves would be freed as soon as possible. All they had to do know was wait for Hammond to do what Alex believed he would do and seek out Sophie.

***

It was a day later when Alex received a call from Emma, telling him that Hammond had just left for a meeting, but he wouldn't say with whom, and he was far more agitated than normal. It thrilled Alex to know that Hammond was as predictable as he thought. The four of them gathered together and made their way to

80

Hammond's bar, where Anne and Alex caught the scent of him. They followed it through the city towards the forest. The road disappeared into bracken and grass, and they had to leave the car behind. It had been a strange sight to see Alex leaning his head out of the window at every possible opportunity to ensure that he didn't lose the scent.

Now that they were closer the scent was stronger, but there was something else too, something familiar.

"She's here," Anne said in an icy tone. "And she's not alone."

The group crept through the forest until they heard voices. The noises came to Alex and Anne sooner than they did to Ben and Amelia. They hid behind a bush and peeked through. Hammond was there, waving his arms wildly as he spoke to Sophie. She seemed impassive, standing with her hands clasped behind her back, her hair locked in a tight ponytail.

She was flanked by two guards.

"What are we going to do?" Amelia asked in a hushed whisper.

"We'll take care of them." Anne said. Her eyes flared with anger at the guards who were dressed in black, a reminder of the ones who had torn their packs apart. Alex grinned as he and his mother shifted at the same time, becoming something more than human, more than a wolf. They raced forward in a streak, quicker than the guards could react. Bullets sprayed across the ground, kicking up clods of dirt.

Anne and Alex lunged at the same time, subduing the enemies. Alex used his strength to bring one down to the ground. He slashed his claws into the man's chest. There was a groan and a sickening sound as he collapsed, and rolled away, gasping for breath, clutching his throat. A few moments passed and then he was still. Anne was filled with fury and leaped off the ground. The guard she targeted looked shocked. There was a moment where he was frozen in fear. Perhaps if he had moved quickly, he would have been able to bring his gun around and fire at her, but the moment's hesitation cost him dear. By the time he had swung his gun around Anne was upon him. The guard managed to get one shot off, but it burst harmlessly into a tree.

The guard yelped as Anne leaped on him, sinking her jaws into his throat. Blood burst out in a thick wave, and crimson rain fell onto the ground. The guard crumpled in a heap and choked on his own blood. The gun fell harmlessly to his side, his hand limply grasping it. Anne lifted her head back and howled loudly, blood dripping from her fangs. It did not avenge all the sorrow or all the people who died, but it did go some way to satisfying her blood lust.

The two wolves turned their beady gazes onto Sophie, who stood with her hands clasped behind her back, as though none of this fazed her at all. Hammond, on the other hand, was a quivering wreck. He held his hands up in supplication and his gaze darted between Anne and Alex, unsure which of the wolves he should have been more fearful of. The wolves snarled as they flanked Sophie. The feral, savage part of Alex's mind told him to kill her now, to kill them both for all the pain they had spread. The part of him that Hammond had trained whined and sneered and gave tempting whispers to tear Hammond apart for everything, for the chains and the beatings and for making Alex think that he was nothing but a brute, a monster.

And yet there was another part of him that knew it was the wrong thing to do, even though it felt so right. There was a wisdom in his wolf soul, one that spoke to prudence and patience. He wondered if his mother would feel the same. Even though she had not been trained as a fighter by Hammond, she had been kept captive for a long time and it would be understandable if she gave into the bloodlust that surged through his mind. However, she still held some wisdom in her soul, and the two wolves transformed back into their human form. The air became duller, and the sweet pain bloomed in Alex's body as he felt his essence transform. The process was so difficult to describe. It was more about feelings than words.

When it was over, he and his mother glared at Sophie, and he was unsettled by how calm she was.

***

"Don't hurt us! Please, I won't do anything. I wasn't going to do anything Alex I promise. Please, we can work out a deal here," Hammond babbled, looking to each of them in turn, fear etched on his face. Alex had always known him to project strength, but now he was a man who had been stripped of all his authority and all his power. He was nothing here, and he looked as though he was ready to promise anything if it would ensure his safety.

"Stop your pathetic whining," Sophie said in a sharp tone, glancing towards him. She only tilted her head slightly. The rest of her body was unmoved, and this made her seem alien and deadly. Although she was human Alex knew well how dangerous she could be, and he wasn't going to give her a chance to prove it.

"Anne, you look well," Sophie added. Anne bristled at the comment, anger twisted on her face.

Alex stepped forward. "We're going to put a stop to your sick experiments Sophie. This is over."

"Over," Sophie said, the corner of her mouth turning up in a slanted smile. "It's far from over. In fact, it's barely just begun. I have only scratched the surface of what is possible. Every day we make new strides, new progress, and now that we have the key I can-"

"The key, you mean my child?" Ben said in a terse voice. His face was heavy with emotion and he stood rigidly, his hands clenched by his side. Sophie turned to him and smiled.

"Yes, you child. The melding of human and wolf DNA, a miracle in other words. The opportunity to study it cannot be passed up. Think of all the knowledge we can glean. Think of the difference it would make to everyone in the world!" her eyes took on a fanatical gleam, the moonlight shining brightly in them, reflecting like two silver pools.

"And it doesn't matter to you what happens to the child, does it? You don't care if it lives or dies. You'll cut it up to learn the secrets and name it all for science. You're a monster," Ben said furiously. Alex watched things carefully. It was a tense situation and he didn't want anything to get out of control. He allowed himself a smirk as he wondered when he had become the reasonable, level-headed one.

Sophie regarded Ben with a cold stare. "You dare call me a monster when these two still walk around, keeping their secrets to themselves? The only monsters here are the ones who refuse to share their gifts with the rest of humanity. Prices must always be paid, and if this child has to give itself up to the needs of science and humanity then so be it. Has it not occurred to you that perhaps this is its purpose? That the only reason it might exist is to point the way to enlightenment and knew knowledge? You should join me. Whether this child lives or dies does not matter, it will always be remembered as a hero. There is nothing that can stop that.

"I refuse to believe that," Ben choked. "We don't have any purpose other than the one we choose for ourselves, and I'm not going to condemn my child to death before it's even had a chance to live. You can't make humanity better by sacrificing an innocent life, a life that hasn't even been given the chance to enter the world. There's nothing you could ever say that could convince me of that." After Ben spoke, his gaze drifted over towards Alex. Alex gave him a little nod of approval and a smile that he hoped would communicate the depth of his love to Ben. From Ben's reaction, he seemed to have the effect he was going for.

But Sophie sighed, a weary, patronizing sigh of someone who wasn't satisfied with anything she was hearing.

"This is why the world is in such a state. It's always being held back by narrow-minded people who can't think of the bigger picture. We should not be slaves to emotion and sentimentality. There are things that need to be done, and it takes the strongest wills to do them!" As she said this, she whipped a pistol around. It must have been nestled in the small of her back. The barrel was pointed straight at Ben.

"Stop! What are you doing? If you kill him, you're going to hurt the baby as well!" Anne yelled. Alex's throat ran dry. Amelia was standing beside Ben, trembling with fear. Hammond whimpered and continued to hold his hands in the air.

"No I won't; I'll just kill the man. I can cut the baby out of him. It won't be as rewarding as if the baby had grown to full term, but I can still make good use out of it." Alex's stomach churned and he knew he had never been in the vicinity of pure evil until now.

"Sophie...what happened to you over the years," Anne said. Her anger seemed to have given way to pity, as though she couldn't believe that the woman standing in front of her was her sister. "I remember you being so angry, but this cruelty...it's not you. It's not the girl I remember. There were moments when you were happy, remember, when we used to walk through the forest and pick flowers and berries? They were good times. How did you lose sight of that? How did you become...this?" Anne looked at Sophie with disdain.

Sophie turned her head and scowled, although she still kept the gun pointed at Ben. Alex thought about rushing Sophie, but he couldn't guarantee that he could move more quickly than her trigger finger, and he wasn't about to take the risk.

"Yes, and you'd always be able to smell the freshest fruit and the sweetest flowers, and you always knew which way to go. I was always trailing behind you Anne. That's what you don't understand. That's what it has been like for me all these years. You've always been ahead of me in everything we've done. And when we went for those walks, they always ended up with me being left alone because you ran off. Being a human was never good enough for you. You always had to shift and run off with the rest of the pack, while I just watched. How do you think that made me feel? That's what all of humanity feels. It's time for a change in the world. Nobody should feel how I was made to feel. Nobody should have to do that. I am going to be the bridge between our two worlds and that bridge is going to be built on science."

"And how many bodies are going to be piled under that bridge?" Anne asked icily, cutting through her sister's diatribe. Sophie's face had flushed and her calm tone had given way to agitated words, although now that Anne interrupted her, she realized that she had lost her composure and gathered herself again.

"Progress cannot be stopped. You should know that more than anyone Anne. This is inevitable. Eventually someone is going to come along and discover the secret of the wolves, so it might as well be me."

"We've managed to keep ourselves a secret for long enough. If you hadn't grown up in our pack you wouldn't have been able to find us," Anne said.

"Perhaps not, but it was only a matter of time. With how quickly the world is moving and how fast civilization is spreading out, soon there won't be a part of the world that remains untouched. The wolves will be sought out and then their gifts will be claimed. I just want to make sure I'm the one to do it. Now stand back and let me get my birthright. Ben, come back with me. We have unfinished business."

"I'm not going anywhere with you. I'm not going to let my child be a part of your experiments. If you're going to kill me then just go ahead, but I'm betting you won't because-"

Ben called her bluff, but Sophie wasn't bluffing. She squeezed the trigger and there was a loud flash, followed by a bang. Alex's heart broke and the world seemed to shatter at the sound of the gunshot. As soon as he realized what was happening, he moved as quickly as he could, embracing every primal part of him to give him an advantage. He shifted in mid-air, his skin thickening into the hide of a wolf. He roared as he threw himself in the path of the bullet, and then he cried out in pain as he felt searing heat punch his shoulder. He fell to the ground and winced, clutching his wound. At the same time, Anne had gone for her sister, wrestling the gun away, and punching her in the face instead of turning into a wolf.

Chapter Ten

Things hadn't exactly gone to plan so far. When Sophie had fired there was a moment that had stretched out for all eternity, and Ben knew he would have to live with his mistake of calling Sophie's bluff. He felt like such a fool. He twisted his body to try and cradle the impact and protect his child, but he knew that he had let the baby down. He had failed as a parent and there would be one fewer beautiful thing in the world. He had just about enough time for his heart to break before everything would end, he had just enough time to say goodbye to the child he would never meet.

But as tears welled in his eyes, he saw a black shadow looming across his path. The bullet should have hit him, but it didn't. Instead, Alex was on the ground, clutching his shoulder. Ben fell down beside him, listening to the cries of agony. Ben had half-shifted into a wolf. The bullet had hit a patch of fur, and blood as black as the night flowed out. Alex writhed and his legs kicked out. He placed his paw on the wound, putting as much pressure on it as he could. Ben put his hand over the paw and pressed down as well, adding to the pressure.

"Get down here and help him!" he barked to Hammond, who quickly fell to his knees and nodded. Anne handed Sophie's gun to Amelia after twisting it out of Sophie's grip. Sophie sunk to her knees and looked groggy, nursing her jaw from where Anne had punched her. Amelia took the gun and held it to Sophie, and then swung it towards Hammond.

"We have to get him to the hospital!" Ben cried.

"No, we have to move forward with the plan," Anne said.

"The plan? There is no plan anymore! The only plan is to save Ben," he screamed, aghast that Anne would dare to sacrifice her son.

"He's going to be fine. His wolf spirit will heal him," Anne said. "We won't get a better chance to get into Black Gate. This is our only chance." Ben knew she was speaking sense, but to think of tearing himself away from Alex was abhorrent. "It's what he would want," she added. Ben thought about how adamant Alex had been about saving the pack and he knew she was right. He pressed his lips together and composed himself. He had to be strong for Ben now, and for their child.

He nodded and rose up, moving towards Anne.

"Amelia, you keep that gun trained on them both. If either of them moves, shoot them," Ben said.

"There's too much blood! I can't stop all of it," Hammond said.

Ben looked down at the blood seeping between Hammond's fingers, but he didn't much care. "Just keep pressure on the wound. If he dies now, I'm going to hold you personally responsible."

"I didn't shoot him!" Hammond cried, but Ben didn't much care. He was already striding towards Sophie, pulling her laboratory coat away from her shoulders. She didn't offer much resistance, as her eyes were locked on the gun that Amelia was holding.

Ben handed the coat to Anne and then deprived Sophie of her ID card.

"I see what you're doing. Do you really think you're going to be able to pass for me? You won't be able to get five feet in Black Gate without someone realizing that something is wrong. You might be able to turn into a wolf Anne, but you can never turn into me."

"I'll do a better job that you think. I know you better than you suspect Sophie. Despite what you might believe I was there during your childhood. I did try and make life better for you. I did try and include you. It's not my fault that you couldn't be what you wanted to be, but that doesn't mean you couldn't have been something else. You're the smartest person I know Sophie. If you had put your efforts into something else, you could have done great work in the world."

"You stole it from me. You stole it before I was born and the only way for me to tip the scales of justice back again is to steal it from another," she ranted. Her words were raw and her eyes dripped with anger. Even though she was on her knees Ben was still wary of her, and he wished that Alex hadn't been hurt so that he could keep a closer eye on her. He didn't like the idea of leaving Amelia with Hammond and Sophie around, but he didn't have a choice. Anne took care of things again, this time by placing a knee in the side of Anne's head, knocking her to the ground with a whimper.

"That's for Owen," Anne said. Ben assumed that Owen was Alex's father. He nodded to Anne as she fasted the ID belt and arranged her hair to match Sophie's. Then, they walked towards Black Gate, hearts thundering with fear as they were both returning to the site of their capture, where horrible things had done to them and they hadn't been sure if they would ever escape. Ben felt a lump form in his throat as the fortress loomed in front of them, but he tried his best to quell the feeling for the sake of what he wanted to accomplish.

***

As they approached Black Gate, they looked at each other.

"We get in and we get out as quickly as possible," Ben said. "We have to make it back to them before anything else can go wrong."

"Don't worry; I don't plan on staying here for one moment longer than is necessary. It's bad enough having to be back here at all. There were times when I never thought I would be free."

"You are now, and we're not going to let that change."

Anne turned to him and smiled. "Alex is lucky to have found someone like you, someone strong. I know that you will take care of him."

"I didn't feel strong back there. I was so stupid to antagonize her. It almost ended me and the child's life. I'm worried this is all wrong. Maybe Ben was right and I shouldn't go into Black Gate."

"We can't second guess ourselves for the sake of our children. We have to keep doing what's right and

92

leading by example. You have done everything to keep your child safe Ben. Some people think that children and loved ones are a weakness because you always have to think of others, but actually I think it can allow us to find hidden reserves of strength. I think I would have died had I not been spurred on by the thought of seeing Alex again. Sophie always taunted me with what she had done with him. Sometimes she said that he had been released by another scientist and was safely out of her clutches to give me hope. Other times she said that he was still at Black Gate and was screaming loudly. Then there were times when she said that I would never see him again. That was the only time when I believed her."

"But she was wrong about that. Just like the way she's been wrong about everything else."

"Yes, and I do wonder what happened to her...I always tried my best to try and include her. I wanted to show her that it didn't matter whether she was a wolf or not; she was still part of the pack. But the pack didn't seem to matter to her. When she looked at me, she only saw the wolf. She only saw the things that she couldn't be and couldn't have. I always feel like there's something I should have done differently."

"You can't help some people," Ben said. He wasn't sure if it would prove to be a help or not. Anne didn't say anything in reply for they were at the entrance to Black Gate and they didn't want to risk being overheard. Anne drew in her breath and shook out her hands and then adopted the same cool, cruel visage that Sophie had.

"I think it would be best if you acted scared of me," she said. Ben nodded and hung his head. It wasn't too much of an ask to act scared because it was how he naturally felt. All he had to do was let it show.

"Let's see how this goes," Anne said as she swiped her keycard against the entrance. The gates lurched open and the guard at the gate greeted her. She nodded sharply and continued walking, holding her head up straight and focusing her gaze directly in front of her in the hope that nobody would feel inclined to speak with her. As it happened Sophie was the kind of woman who didn't have time for meaningless conversations, so nobody bothered them. They strode through Black Gate. The corridors and the stale smell were all too familiar. Ben's heart clutched in his chest. Anne added to the performance by muttering and pushing Ben along, as though he was nothing to her but a lab rat.

As soon as they reached her office they relaxed and breathed a sigh of relief. The façade fell from Anne's face and she smiled at him, apologizing for the way she had acted. Ben told her not to worry as it was all part of the plan.

"Are you going to be okay here? I need to go and get the wolves," she asked.

"Are you going to be okay? What are you going to do once they're free? I don't think the guards are going to be too shy about shooting the prisoners."

"We'll get out as fast as we can, spread through the forest. They might be weak, but they'll be eager to stretch their legs again. They'll prefer to be running anyway. A chance of escape is better than being held captive. If they wait here, they're only suffering a slow death."

Ben and Anne nodded to each other before they went their separate ways. Ben started to rifle through drawers and pulled out as many files as he could, taking pictures and videos of as much as he could. Once he was done in Sophie's office he went into the room where he had been held. Nausea swam in the pit of his stomach and flashes of trauma burst in his mind as he approached the table upon which he had been restrained. As he reached out to touch it, he closed his eyes and could see himself there, quivering and shuddering in fear. He brought his hand back and took pictures, documenting the restraints and the medical tools. Then, he moved further through the facility and took a picture of the cage in which Anne had been held. There was so much horror in this place and he was filled with a righteous anger to take it all down. It wasn't right that a place such as this should exist, where a mad scientist like Sophie could poke and prod her captives without having to adhere to any kind of laws or regulations.

Suddenly an alarm rang out and Ben knew it was time for him to leave. He heard the thundering footsteps of guards clattering down corridors, ready to prevent the escape of the wolves. Ben snuck out, moving through the shadows as best he could. When he tasted air, the freedom was sweet but he didn't stop running. He knew he couldn't let himself get complacent. Out of the facility he saw streaks rushing into the forest with squadrons of guards chasing after them. The air was alive with howls and Ben smiled. The wolves were free and he had all the information he needed to bring Cyan down.

It wasn't long after this that he and Anne reunited. She was in wolf form, and came staggering towards him, shifting back into human form before his eyes. She smiled, although she looked tired.

"That was something," she said. "Did you get everything you need?"

"I think so. Did you free them all?"

"I did. There were a few who got caught by the guards before they left, but most of them made it out. They're trusting themselves in nature now. Hopefully the woods will hide them."

"Do you think you'll ever see them again?"

"Oh yes, we'll reunite eventually. It's just a matter of time. But for now, we must spread ourselves wide to make ourselves harder to catch." She and Ben walked back through the forest to where the others were waiting for them, but as they approached Anne sniffed the air and a concerned look came upon her face.

"What's wrong?" Ben asked.

"I'm not sure..." she said, but they soon found out. Standing by their group was a man, flanked by two guards. When Ben and Anne approached the man turned and greeted them with a thin smile. His features were pale and plain, as though the sun had never touched his skin. He wore a suit well and held himself rigidly. Ben glanced towards Alex, who was sitting up now. Amelia was beside him, and Hammond continued to cower. Sophie was groggily getting to her knees, and Ben was afraid that victory was going to slip through their hands.

Chapter Eleven

The man towered above them. Alex's mind was still hazy. Pain bloomed in his shoulder, although by now his features had shifted back into a human and the blood was not flowing as freely as it had done before. Hammond had actually done his duty and remained by Alex's side, keeping pressure on the wound. His hands were stained with blood, although now he looked ashen at the man.

"Well, it seems as though you have caused quite the little stir in our area. It's very resourceful. You should be commended for causing as much damage as you have. My name is Mr. Anderson, and I'm here to tell you that what you're doing has to stop." He spoke in a calm, confident tone, although Alex figured that it was easy to be confident with two armed guards flanking him.

"And why should we do that?" Ben asked.

"Because if you don't, I'll kill you. It's as simple as that really," he said, and then he smiled again. "But thankfully for you I am a businessman rather than an assassin and I'm here to make a deal."

"What kind of deal?" Alex asked.

Sophie pushed herself to her feet and scowled, rubbing the side of her head.

"We can't make a deal with them. There's only one thing I'm interested in and there's nothing they want. We have to take it by force," she said. Mr. Anderson glared at her.

"Be quiet," he said sternly. Alex was shocked to hear Sophie being spoken to like that. So far, she had been the one in control, but in a corporation like Cyan there were always more important people. She looked cowed and glared at the ground. Alex felt a small sense of triumph at her reaction, but he was also wary of this man. He turned his gaze from Sophie and looked at the rest of them.

"I'm aware that you know what happens in Black Gate. I must assure you that whatever has happened behind Black Gate's doors is entirely the responsibility of this scientist and Cyan does not condone any behavior like this. We are taking immediate measures to make up for her mistakes and there will be a full internal investigation into her practices."

"Yes, there will be, and there will be an external one as well. People are going to learn what happened here," Ben said defiantly. Mr. Anderson licked his lips and tilted his head. He took one step forward. It was a small gesture, and yet it seemed to be a monumental stride.

"Actually, we would rather that didn't happen," Mr. Anderson said. "I know that as journalists you value the truth above all else, but at Cyan we value our reputation too. We would prefer you not disclose anything about what happened here."

"There's no way of you squirming out of this," Ben said. "I have everything I need."

"And I'm going to need you to give it back," Mr. Anderson said. "Otherwise the consequences will be most…unappetizing."

"I thought you said you weren't a killer," Amelia said.

"I'm not, but they are," Mr. Anderson said. The guards flexed their arms, showing off their heavy rifles. "I would much rather it didn't come to that though as we are not in the habit of taking these measures to deal with our problems, but I want to assure you that we are going to question Dr. Malone thoroughly to ensure that what she did never happens again."

"No… you can't! I was doing this for you, for all of humanity!" Sophie, yelled, but her pleas fell on deaf ears. Alex knew the truth though, as he suspected they all did. Sophie hadn't done this for anyone but herself. Mr. Anderson glared at her again, and it was enough to keep her quiet.

"You can leave in peace and return to your lives. All I require is that you do not talk about anything that happened here and you destroy the evidence you acquired tonight."

Ben scoffed. "Why would I do that? We hold all the cards here."

"This isn't about cards. This is about guns. If you don't take my deal there might be a tragedy, and I'm not just talking about with you. I'm talking about all of the…subjects who are currently running through the forest. I could devote incredible resources to the task of hunting them down and making sure that none of them make it out alive, or I could call my men off and dismantle Black Gate. The choice is yours," he said.

It was an awful choice. Each of them wanted to bring Cyan down, but it almost seemed too big to fall. Alex glanced at Ben. They shared an unspoken bond, and they knew what they had to do. They had come here with the prime goal of freeing the pack. If they gave their lives up now, they wouldn't be accomplishing anything. At least if they lived to fight another day, they might have one more chance to take Cyan down.

With a heavy heart Ben pulled out his phone and showed Mr. Anderson that he was deleting everything. Mr. Anderson nodded and pursed his lips.

"I'm glad that you are reasonable people. I'm happy that we could come to some arrangement. I apologize for the trouble that Dr. Malone caused. I will see to it that the same thing never happens again. Of that you have my personal guarantee," he said. He gestured to his guards. They pulled Sophie up and dragged her away. She protested and howled, struggling against them with all her might, but she could not resist them. She looked to her sister for salvation, but Anne had no sympathy left for her, and let Sophie be taken away. She faded into the darkness, and they never heard from her again.

***

"Well, you made the right choice there. There's no messing with something as big as Cyan. Better to escape with your lives than try and give them a bloody nose," Hammond said, wiping his hands on the grass.

"I can't believe they're just going to get away with it," Amelia said, her face ashen with disbelief. Ben moved to Alex and helped him stand. Pain still throbbed, but his strength was returning to him and although the world lurched around him, he could still stand with a little support.

"We have to take the victories when we can," Ben said. "We escaped with our lives and we freed the wolves. We might not get Cyan today, but we'll work on getting them tomorrow, and the next day, and the one after that. Black Gate will be no more and Sophie won't be doing her horrible experiments. I know it might not feel like it at the moment, but we did some good today, and it's important to remember that." Alex leaned his head against Ben's shoulder, proud of the speech and the outlook on life. They *had* done well, and at least they were together. At least they could return home and look to the future, knowing that their baby was safe from pursuit.

"What are we going to do with him?" Amelia asked, looking at Hammond.

"Well, there's nothing to do with me really. I'm harmless, you know, I never actually *worked* for Cyan; I was just a middleman really, and of course I didn't know the extent to which she was torturing you. I just thought you were some crazy experiment, and we had some good times didn't we Alex? You know, my offer still stands. If you want to come back and work at the bar you can have any position you want. I mean it, anything. You can work behind the bar, you can be a bouncer, hell, you can even fight again if you want," Hammond said.

Alex merely glared at him.

"I'm not going back with you Hammond. I have another life now. You can make your own way home. And Hammond, be good to your wife, and don't get up to anything like the fighting pit. I might come by some time just to make sure you're behaving yourself and don't forget; I know where the chains are."

Hammond looked agog and he chased after them as they walked away, not believing that they would actually leave him there. Alex glared back and snarled at him, telling him to keep his distance. Then Hammond did get the message. In the distance the sound of a howl could be heard. Hammond was stricken with fear and ran off in the direction of the city, fleeing as quickly as he could.

"Well, there's another problem taken care of. Now we just have to get you fixed up," Anne said, glancing at Alex's wound. Although he had turned into his human form, the area of the wound was still the form of a wolf. Thick fur appeared on the skin, and so it didn't seem that they could go to a hospital. But then Anne had the idea of seeing Dr. Monroe. She was perhaps the only one in the city who could help them without raising questions.

***

Dr. Monroe rolled her eyes when the group appeared at her doorstep. When she saw the bullet hole, she looked shocked and welcomed them in. She gave Alex a herbal remedy to numb the pain,

103

something that Ben was wary of, but Alex didn't think she meant harm to him. She pulled the bullet out and then smeared some thick cream over the wound. It stung and it had a greenish tint to it, as well as a bitter, pungent aroma. Alex arched his eyebrows, and the rest of them all took a step back from him.

"I told you not to mess with Cyan. This is what you get," Julia muttered.

"At least Sophie isn't performing her experiments. Black Gate is going to be shut down," Anne said.

"I'm sure something just as bad is going to crop up somewhere," Amelia said bitterly.

Julia studied her. "I learned a long time ago that if you hold onto fights you can't win it's only going to tear you up inside. You lot fared far better than plenty of other people. Mostly Cyan chews everyone up and spits them out. You came out intact, and you should feel lucky." She cleaned her hands, sighed for a moment, and then her expression and tone softened. "I have been thinking about what you said though," she glanced towards Ben. "Perhaps I have been too eager to lose myself in plants. I should not forget the reason why I became involved with Cyan in the first place was to improve humanity. With all that I saw along the way, I forgot that, and I became so scared...I want to help you now. You are going to need help when it comes to giving birth to the child. I doubt any hospital would allow you to go in without having a full investigation about how such a thing could happen. I am sorry that things with Cyan didn't go the way you hoped, but at least we can all move forward now," Julia said.

Ben and Alex thanked her for the offer, although Alex could tell that Ben wasn't entirely comfortable with the idea. As badly as the ointment smelled, it was having a healing effect and the skin was already beginning to feel soothed. The group left Julia's house trying to hold onto the feeling of victory, but it couldn't help feeling like defeat. Although the wolves had been freed Cyan were still able to go and do whatever they liked. But some battles were too big to win and they had to take triumph where they could. As Alex gazed towards the stars, he thought of the other wolves running free after years of being in captivity, and he knew he had done well and he should be proud of what he accomplished. Then, he looked towards his mother and the man he loved. He had brought them all together and they were a family again. His memory was filled, and he would never again have to wonder who he was.

Chapter Twelve

"And that's it. That's what happened. We have nothing. All that time, all those resources, and we have nothing to show for it. I'm sorry William. I really thought we could put together a story that would have everyone reading our paper. It's not how any of us wanted it to turn out," Ben said after he had explained everything to William. Amelia was sitting in the chair besides Ben, looking even more forlorn.

"You know, it was always going to be a hard sell anyway. Sometimes in this career, you get to learn things that you can't ever share with other people and you can't ever prove. It's just the nature of the beast. But look, you both did good work and I'm proud of you. I know this wasn't how any of us wanted it to end up, but there was some good to come out of it. Black Gate has been dismantled. The doctor there has been shamed and fired and stricken from her profession. You stopped whatever was going on there, and for that you should be proud," he said with a kindly smile.

"But nobody is going to know the truth," Amelia said. "Ben had so much. We could have buried them."

"Maybe, maybe not. Companies like Cyan always have tricks up their sleeve and they always have people willing to bend the rules in their favor. If you had gone through with it we'd be up to our eyeballs in lawsuits, you'd be hunted and targeted by the people they employ to fix their problems, and in the end you might not have made any progress anyway. You win some, you lose some, and in the end, we just have to keep on fighting as best we can."

Ben shook his head. He hated to admit that William was right, but there seemed to be nothing more they could do.

"Besides, in my experience the truth always has a way of coming out. It might not make much difference to you now but in the end, people will know about Cyan and they'll face justice."

Ben wasn't entirely sure whether to believe William or not, but he nodded anyway and thanked William for all the backing he had given them. It would have been easy for William to shut up shop and refuse to even consider the possibility of investigating Cyan, but he hadn't. He was a good man, and Ben hoped that he would still have the same measure of integrity when he was William's age.

He and Amelia stepped outside into the crisp air.

"So, what are you going to do with your time off?" Ben asked. William had been kind enough to grant them a vacation after their intense investigation.

"I don't know. I might take a trip somewhere, get out of the city for a while. I still have the feeling that someone is watching me and I just can't shake it," Amelia said, glancing around furtively.

"That sounds like a good idea. You deserve all the rest I can get. Look, I just wanted to say thank you for everything you did. I know that this wasn't your story. You went above and beyond, and I know that if you hadn't gone to get Alex I wouldn't have been rescued from Black Gate. You're a good friend Amelia."

"The best," Amelia said with a grin. She punched Ben on the arm playfully. "You're very welcome, and you'll just have to remember that you owe me, big time."

"You got it," he replied with a grin, having no doubt that she would call in that favor one day, and he would repay it gladly. "Just make sure you're back in time for the birth."

"Oh don't worry; I wouldn't miss that for the world," Amelia said. She waved at him as she turned away and walked home, leaving Ben to face the prospect of returning home himself.

***

"Ben, I'm glad I caught you," Anne said. Alex turned away, hiding his face. Anne wiped her eyes.

"What's going on?" Ben asked.

"I just had a word with Alex and explained to him what I'm going to do next. I have to go out there to try and find them Ben. I have to find the wolves and rebuild the pack. Believe me, there's nothing I would prefer to do than stay here with you and help you prepare for the child, but we must make the pack strong again. After Black Gate they all fled. They'll be scared and mistrustful. Without help they might not be able to understand their place in the world again. I must help them learn, as you helped Ben learn, and as you both helped me." She smiled sadly. "My sister has done much damage and I must do my best to repair as much of it as possible."

"Will you be back?" Ben asked, glancing towards Alex, worried for him.

Anne smiled widely. "Of course. I want to bring the pack together so that when your child is born, we can welcome them into the pack and you as well. It will be strong again, as it was before Sophie divided us."

She hugged Ben and then hugged Alex one more time before disappearing out of the door in a whirl of tears. Alex fell into Ben's arms and hugged him tightly.

"It's going to be okay," Ben said.

"I know, it's just that I spent so long aching to have her back and then I did, and now she's gone. I know it's something she needs to do and I know that I'm going to see her again, it's just that part of me is really scared to see her leave."

"Like you say, we'll see her again," Ben reassured him, kissing him on the forehead.

"How did things go at the office?"

"Well it was okay. William had some words of wisdom and he gave me and Amelia some time off to collect ourselves. I'll have to start thinking of the next story to write, although I won't be going after a corporation again."

"No, I think that's enough for one lifetime."

"I just hate that they're still out there." Ben moved towards the window and gazed out at the huge skyscraper that dwarfed the city. "It's like they're mocking us, as though they get to play by their own rules."

"It's always been the same," Alex said, tugging at Ben's shoulder, pulling his gaze away from the window. "But we have to remember that we helped people. We can't always win all the fights we take part in, but we at least gave them a bloody nose. It's time for us to enjoy our lives now. We can put this all behind us."

Ben nodded and sighed. As he exhaled, he felt as though he was releasing a lot of tension. He kissed Alex softly and let the feeling linger before he recoiled and coughed.

"I want to be romantic, but it's so hard to do when you have that on there," he glanced to the ointment that had been spread over Alex's chest. He had put a fresh dressing on that morning, but it didn't smell any nicer than the first one. Alex laughed.

"Well, how about you come and help me wash it off," he said. He took Ben's hand and led him into the shower, turning on the faucet. Steam spilled out and filled the room.

****

The water hissed and warmth tingled upon Ben's flesh. Alex smirked as he started to undress, peeling his shirt away button by button, teasing Ben with the anticipation of it all. He shrugged it off and the shirt fell to the floor. Ben breathed in appreciation of Alex's muscles. The swelling biceps and the wide torso looked as though they had been sculpted by a master. Alex held Ben's gaze as he unbuttoned his jeans and pulled them off, before pushing down his underwear as well. He stood there stark naked, with his manhood on full display, and Ben felt as though he was in heaven. The steam rose around Alex, enveloping him in a thin mist, as though he was some ethereal god come down from the heavens to bless Ben.

"Your turn," Alex said. His whisper was filled with intent. Ben fumbled with his clothes as he tore them off and soon enough, he was standing there exposed as well, every inch of him twitching with fervent arousal. Tendrils of steam wrapped around him, acting as though they had a mind of their own, pulling Ben towards Alex. Alex opened his arms and welcomed Ben into him, pressing his body close. Alex was a few inches taller than Ben, so Ben tilted his head up and smiled. Alex kissed him softly and there was a comforting moan as Ben let the pleasure surge through him, as hot as the water that hissed in the shower.

Alex took his hand and led him into the shower. The water crashed around them in powerful jets, slamming against their skin. Alex and Ben kept close together, trying to get as much of the water against their bodies as possible. Ben's heart thudded inside as he smeared his hands across Alex's chest, wiping the ointment away. It fell in great clumps to the floor and was swallowed by the drain. They laughed as they watched it disappear and then began washing to rid themselves of the pungent aroma. They each took handfuls of the soap and rubbed it over each other's bodies. It frothed and bubbled and soon it was as though they were standing on clouds, for all the foam rested around their feet. Their hair was matted to their face and water trickled down their cheeks and bodies. They tickled and teased each other, having been intimate enough with each other to know secret sweet spots. They yelped and gasped, and then they fell into silence as they kissed.

Fingers dug into supple skin. Alex's body bristled with pleasure and passion as he pinned Ben against the wall. His strength was such that Ben was actually lifted off his toes, and for a moment it felt as though he was floating. His hands moved quickly around Alex's body, frantically. They dove down and felt his manhood. Ben groaned as he felt the size throbbing in his palm. He sank to his knees and began to pleasure Alex with his mouth. He looked up and water peppered his eyes, blurring his vision, but all he could see was Alex towering above him, looking like a god.

Ben drew back as his mouth filled with water and he let out a choking cough. Alex grinned and took his turn to suck Ben. Ben ran his hands along his chest, as though he was directing the crackling energy that surged inside him. He felt Alex's fingers slide around the hidden parts of his body, and then suddenly Alex was inside him, preparing for him. Ripples of pleasure shimmered through Ben's mind and his knees went weak. He pressed his back against the wall to steady himself, and only Alex prevented him from melting. Water continued to cascade down over his skin as Alex returned to his feet. He turned Ben around, and a smile spread over Ben's face.

Alex's arms coiled around him like lustful serpents and held him tightly as he plunged into him. Ben welcomed him, feeling the huge, masculine strength stretching him. He gasped as the pain and pleasure blurred into one intoxicating sensation. It lanced through him and set his soul on fire as Alex thrust into him. The strong limbs kept Ben in place. He opened his palms and steadied himself against the wall, making sure that he didn't fall. But he knew he was safe with Alex. The water crashed against his neck as did Alex's breath. Ben closed his eyes as he enjoyed all the sensations that came rushing through him.

He twisted his neck back to kiss Alex. Their lips brushed against each other before Ben felt Alex getting deeper inside him than he ever had before. Ben's mouth formed a wide 'O' shape and his body almost bent double as the pleasure became almost too much to bear. He was lost in a world of pleasure and heat and lust. It was overwhelming and left him delirious, but it also burned away all the anguish and the bitterness that remained in his soul. It reminded him that no matter what, he was a winner because he had Alex.

It was at that moment that both men came.

***

The shuddering bliss made Ben tremble. Alex pressed his head against the back of Ben's neck. Ben felt the sharp heat surging with him. It was hotter than even the water, and far more satisfying. The haze filled his mind and he breathed deeply. His heart hammered, and when he opened his eyes he saw the remnants of his own lust sliding down, mixing with the foamy water, before it was sucked away, just as the shower cleansed away all their negative feelings.

113

Ben turned around and wrapped his arms around Alex, kissing him deeply. He gazed into Alex's eyes.

"I love you," he said, "more than anything, and I know that I'm never going to stop loving you."

"Good, because I have no plans to ever stop," Alex said, sealing his promise with a kiss.

They turned off the water and stepped out of the shower. They dried themselves with soft towels, taking time to be gentle and sensual with each other. They kissed and caressed each other, before walking towards the bedroom, still naked, and wrapping themselves up in a cocoon of love. They talked about all the good things in their lives and everything happy that they wanted to happen in the future. It went some way to preventing them from falling into sorrow, and as they lay there naked, with nothing separating them except for air, they basked in their love and felt utterly happy. Ben didn't feel despair about the lack of justice with regards to Cyan, he only looked forward to meeting the future with Alex.

And what a future it would be.

Epilogue

Many months later...

The past months had been difficult for Alex and Ben. As Ben's stomach had swollen, he had to stay hidden from the world, which meant Alex had to run all the errands. Alex had some tips for Ben as he was used to hiding himself, but they didn't do much to help as Ben started to get cabin fever. Amelia helped out where she could, and towards the end Anne had returned, declaring that she had succeeded in gathering the wolves and reforming the pack. They had decided to settle on the other side of the city this time, as far from Black Gate as possible.

The news about the dismantling of Black Gate had not been as momentous as any of them would have liked. It was quite likely that most of the common people wouldn't have known anything about it, and all the ordeal faded as quietly as a whisper.

As the pregnancy continued, Ben's emotions became more erratic and there were some days when he wept uncontrollably, while at other times his temper got the better of him and he snapped at Alex, although he apologized straight away. When the baby was due, he was ready for it to come out, although there was a lot of fear as well as this was never something he had prepared for. He was filled with trepidation as he went to Julia's house. She gave him something for the pain, which he only took at the insistence of Alex, as Ben was still wary of accepting anything from her.

However, as soon as he drank it, he relaxed and was grateful that he had something to take the edge off. The birth was difficult and complicated, and it would have been much safer to have it happen in a hospital, but they couldn't allow anyone to know the truth of the matter. Thankfully Julia was skilled and knew what she was doing, even if her specialty was plants. When she lifted the baby boy out, she handed him to Alex and Ben, marveling at the miracle child. Both men smiled and gazed at the child in awe, before kissing each other. Ben felt tired and his body ached, but he had enough about him to take the child into his arms and swaddle him in a blanket.

"He looks just like you," Alex said.

Ben grinned. "I was about to say that he looks just like you."

"I guess he looks like us," Alex smiled back, and kissed Ben on the head.

"What's his name?" Julia asked.

"Peter," Ben replied. Julia nodded. There was a strange look on her face and she seemed to be struggling with something, although neither Ben nor Alex were sure what, and frankly they didn't care as they had far too much on their mind already. Their son seemed to shine with radiant light, and they were all too willing to be blinded by him. Little Peter was the most beautiful thing they had ever seen, and neither of them knew anything like it.

They returned home and over the following few days they received visitors to the house. Amelia was enthusiastic about being an honorary aunt, and she already spoiled Peter with gifts and affection. Anne came as well, wanting to meet the child alone before he was presented to the pack. She cooed over him, and to see her in this element made it difficult to believe that she had been held captive for such a long time. But although she and the others, including Alex and Ben, would never forget their trauma, they could at least move on from it and find their way to happiness. They had seen how a soul could become twisted and bitter with hatred in Sophie, and none of them were going to follow her example.

It was a time of great joy, and it was only going to get better.

A few days after this something happened that surprised them all. A group of noted scientists and other professionals came out to expose Cyan's shady business dealings and illegal, unethical practices. Since Julia had been so adamant about remaining tight-lipped, Alex and Ben were puzzled as to why she would come forward now. She would later contact them to say that seeing Peter being born had persuaded her to make a stand because there were going to be innocent people like him that would not have a voice. She knew that if things had gone differently Peter might never have entered the world, and she couldn't stand by and let a company get away with things like that. She got in touch with former colleagues and they decided to come forward as a group, deciding that there was safety in numbers and that Cyan would not try and silence them all.

It worked as well. The story blew up and as more truths came to light more people felt empowered to speak out. Suddenly Cyan was on the ropes, flailing to keep its reputation intact.

But Alex and Ben let the story run on its own, for they had something else to occupy their time.

***

It was a dark night and the moon shone full and brightly in the sky, hanging like a paper lantern. Stars twinkled around it, and the moon was bathed in a silver glow. Peter was wrapped tightly in a blanket to protect him from the cold. Alex and Ben walked forward and stood beside Anne, who stood in front of her pack, ready to address them.

"We have been through so much sorrow. We have lost so many who were dear to us, but the pack still remains! And now we have this symbol of a new hope, of a new era. Like so many of you there were times when I thought that we would never be a pack again. My sister did something terrible to us, but she could never take apart what makes us wolves strong. We found a way back to each other because we are bonded, not just by our blood, but by our souls. We are recovering, but we will ensure that nothing like that ever happens again. I pledge to you now that this is the beginning of a new future, and this child is the symbol of that," her voice boomed across the glade and she beckoned for Alex to hand her Peter.

She lifted the child up so that everyone could see.

"Look upon this child and know that your future is secure. Know that we will never forsake each other again, and we will never lose ourselves to the wilderness. Shift now, show your true forms and welcome this child into the pack! Give him the welcome he deserves, the welcome of wolves!"

Her words reverberated into the air and they were powerful enough that they seemed to rise into the sky and join the stars. As Ben watched, the wolves turned into their primal forms and they lifted their snouted faces into the sky, peering at the moon to give it their thanks. Alex shifted beside him as well. The only one who didn't change was Anne, as she still had hold of the child. Although Ben couldn't shift with them, he was still profoundly affected by the ceremony, and he felt deeply connected to them.

The wolves howled in a cacophony. Anne lifted up Peter and the baby began to cry; slowly but surely, the baby's cries became lost in the howl of wolves. He was one of them, and Ben couldn't have been prouder. He stood there in front of the wolves, proud to know that his child was part of a pack. He looked up to the moon as well. Silver light danced upon his face, and he felt blessed.

www.ingramcontent.com/pod-product-compliance
Lightning Source LLC
Chambersburg PA
CBHW071918120726
48001CB00005B/1781